★

TOO CLOSE FOR COMFORT

I sat in the car and thought all the way home. What bothered me was this: Eric Huffman's computer had suffered from a virus. Eric Huffman had given Shane Corbett a place to live. Eric Huffman was dead.

Helen Thorne's computer had suffered from the same virus. Helen Thorne's restaurant had given Shane Corbett a job. Helen Thorne was dead.

Harry Ralston's computer had suffered from the same virus. Harry Ralston had given Shane Corbett a place to live.

I was not happy. Definitely I was not happy.

★

HACKER

LEE MARTIN

WORLDWIDE®

TORONTO • NEW YORK • LONDON
AMSTERDAM • PARIS • SYDNEY • HAMBURG
STOCKHOLM • ATHENS • TOKYO • MILAN
MADRID • WARSAW • BUDAPEST • AUCKLAND

HACKER

A Worldwide Mystery/January 1994

First published by St. Martin's Press, Incorporated.

ISBN 0-373-26135-7

AUTHOR'S NOTE

About seven years ago my son, then sixteen, walked into the house one day and said, "This is Tim. I found him sleeping on the beach. Now he lives with us." And live with us he did, for the next eight months. Avatars of Tim have turned up in several of my books, but never before as a main character. I've really got to dedicate this book to Tim, who will probably never see it.

PROLOGUE

IF I REALLY want to make myself miserable, I can start adding up all the money we have put out on Harry's hobbies, money that—in my opinion at least—could have been spent on better things, like maybe some decent furniture. Let's see, there's the private airplane he now flies about twelve hours a year. Not only was the initial expense mind-boggling at a time when we could least afford it—though I can't think of a time when I would have felt we could afford it—but on top of that we still have to pay hanger rent for it twelve months a year.

There's that camping gear stored in the camper in the back of Harry's pickup truck. Our son Hal does use some of it now and then, but Harry never goes camping anymore. All the same, we had to replace every piece of it after the stuff we had wound up as evidence in a murder trial in New Mexico.

There was the extensive model railroad set, complete with track and scenery, that he got tired of and gave to Hal for Christmas. As Hal never wanted it to start with, it is now gathering dust on a shelf in the garage.

There are his guns, kept, Harry says, for hunting season. Last time he went hunting Vicky wasn't in school yet, and she's now finished high school and secretarial school and has been married long enough to be expecting her second child.

There's all the ham radio equipment, including over a thousand dollars' worth of fancy antenna towering over the house, its mast sunk in a concrete slab in the front yard. The equipment itself is now stacked in crates in the garage, because its place is now occupied with the computer.

Ah, the computer! Harry says the college where he is now working on his MBA *told* him to get the computer. He may well be telling the truth; he usually tells the truth as he sees it. But the college certainly did *not* tell him to spend twenty hours a day playing with the computer. Sometimes I am not certain whether I want to sue the computer for alienation of affection, or simply bash Harry in the head some dark night.

At a glance, I guessed that Eric Huffman had been somewhat the same kind of man. At least I could see, in his garage and this bedroom that he was using as just about everything except a bedroom, considerable evidence of expensive hobbies abandoned and replaced. But I didn't really want to bash Harry in the head, and I didn't figure Clara Huffman had done the bashing in this case. Her shock and grief seemed far more than just conventional.

One thing was certain. Whoever bashed Eric Huffman had done a very thorough job of it, and I didn't expect to get home early today.

And this really wasn't a good day to be late. Not that any day in the last two weeks had been good. In any way. Not since Hal's girlfriend, Lori Hankins, had stepped off the curb behind the downtown library in Fort Worth about three steps before her mother, Policewoman Donna Hankins. Only three steps ahead, but the car that hit her—and kept on going—had knocked her forty feet. As Donna hadn't been able to get the license plate number, it appeared that our chances of locating the driver were nil.

Meanwhile Lori remained at Methodist Hospital, comatose.

Only half an hour earlier I'd sat down at my desk for what I intended to be about five minutes, just long enough to look through my in-basket and see how much of its contents I could safely sneak into somebody else's in-basket before heading for home and a three-day weekend I'd probably spend spelling Donna at Lori's bedside and trying to talk Hal into getting some rest.

"So what's going on?" Dutch Van Flagg asked me, as I industriously rearranged papers.

I shrugged, not wanting to talk about it.

"You don't know what's going on?"

I wanted to scream at him to quit trying to cheer me up. But I didn't. None of it was his fault, and he was trying to cheer me up because he cared. So I managed to wave my right hand around languidly, as I would have done if I'd really felt like joking. "Danged if I know, Dutch. I've given up. Now I just sort of run around in circles and every now and then I scream a little bit."

"Right," Dutch chuckled. "So go and run around in a few more circles. Or is it time to scream right now?"

Gathering up a stack of papers and dumping them casually into Nathan Drucker's basket, I said, "Dutch, old buddy, old friend, old pal, I'm going home. I've been stuck in that blasted witness room ten hours a day for a week and a half."

Which was true. Which had added to the displeasure of the week.

Dutch chuckled again. He had managed to miss out on the blackmail trial that had kept half the Major Case Squad tied up in court for a week and a half. We'd all been tired of it even before it began, the blackmailee being no more outstanding a citizen than the blackmailer, and between the trial and the hospital I had found myself doing laundry at midnight two nights earlier so that I wouldn't be reduced to wearing slacks and a sweatshirt to court. Now that it was over, with the anticipated guilty verdict, I had exactly one thing on my mind, and that was getting home in time to cook supper for my beloved family before dashing back out to the hospital.

Of course, not much of my beloved family would be at home. Or at least not at my home. Both daughters are now married and coping with their own offspring, and Hal, at seventeen, wasn't quite as crazy as he'd been at sixteen. In fact, before Lori's accident, he'd been downright normal—at least, normal for Hal. Now, of course, he was attempting to live at the hospital.

Over a year ago my youngest child, Cameron, had begun to steadfastly refuse to eat baby food at nine months, though I'd had to remove him from the dog's dish several times. Although the pediatrician assured me there really wasn't anything in dog food likely to harm a healthy baby, I found the idea aesthetically displeasing. We—the baby and I—had reached some sort of agreement that he would eat fruit yogurt, scrambled eggs, and mashed bananas, and I would not offer him that kind of stuff that comes in jars with cute labels pasted on them. Fortunately by now, at twenty-one months, he was eating mostly from the table, so I no longer had to plan separate meals for him unless we were having something like steak, and who could afford that?

But this was Friday and I was out of court. I would be taking my day off for New Year's on Monday, over two weeks early—I certainly couldn't take it on New Year's Day itself, as the murder rate tends to be awfully high just then—so I was off for what, in normal conditions, would have been three, count 'em, three glorious, beautiful days when I didn't have to think about police work.

Even if a weekend at the hospital couldn't be considered "normal conditions," I still didn't plan on thinking about police work. I had quite enough to do.

But you know what they say about the best-laid plans of mice and men?

The saying goes for women, too.

So here I stood, at four-thirty in the afternoon, on Friday, the thirteenth (wouldn't you just know it?) of December, looking at my very first ax murder.

I don't throw up at crime scenes, like some people I know, but I definitely wasn't enjoying it.

ONE

DUTCH HAD DRIVEN and I had sulked all the way to the victim's house.

As I sulked, I remembered asking a friend from another department why she'd suddenly decided to leave police work. She'd answered, "Because I realized I wasn't quite human anymore."

"What?" I said, grotesque visions of Robocop running through my head.

"I got a call," she said, "to the stupid, senseless suicide of a fifteen-year-old boy. He was lying on the sidewalk, the pistol still in his hand, and so much gray matter lying around that a traffic man thought the kid had been vomiting, and he asked me if I knew why the kid had been eating oatmeal at seven-thirty at night. I had to explain that was his brains, which he'd literally blown out."

"Yuck," I said.

"Yeah. Yuck, at least. And gross. And a few other expressions like that. But Deb, you know what I was thinking as I looked at him?"

I shook my head. "No. What?"

"I was thinking, 'Why'd the son of a bitch have to blow himself away on *my* shift?' That's what I was thinking. And then I realized that's not the way a human being thinks. And I realized I'd better get out of this business while I still had a chance to get back to being human."

I was perilously near that stage of burnout myself, now. I wasn't thinking about a real live man attacked and hacked to bits as he went about his own peaceful business. I wasn't thinking about the grief, the shock, the horror, of a real live woman arriving home to find her husband hacked to bits.

No, I was busy thinking about me, Deb Ralston, and about my family and my friends and my problems, foremost of which was a sixteen-year-old girl who—assuming she woke up—was very likely one day to become my daughter-in-law.

Unlike my friend who'd left policing, I wasn't even technically on duty or on call. I'd just happened, along with Dutch Van Flagg, to be—unfortunately—in the office when the call came in. And so, with Dutch Van Flagg, I was now at another murder.

I had not been planning on going to a murder this afternoon. What I really wanted to do—between and among feeding the family, cleaning the house, doing the laundry, and catching up on all the other little errands that collect when I'm in court—was to sit beside Lori's bed while Donna—as she had to do, like it or not—went to work. I wanted to sit by Lori's bed and finish crocheting the Christmas tree I had begun sometime in August.

Never mind why I was crocheting a Christmas tree. I have these fits of domesticity. They usually begin about the time the days start to grow shorter—I tend to want to hibernate in the winter, or at least sit by the fire in wool socks—and end sometime in March, when the weather starts looking worth going outdoors in. But when the fits of domesticity are upon me I do strange things.

Like crocheting—or attempting to crochet—green yarn Christmas trees, and pink and blue and purple balls and stars to hang on the big Christmas tree.

Like buying a lap quilting frame, in hope of maybe actually *quilting* that quilt top I started making about twenty-six years ago, when I was a bride living in a sort of trailer park for low-ranked enlisted people on Camp Pendleton Marine Base. (That was before Harry managed to finish college, learn to fly, and thus get a commission. The next time we lived on Camp Pendleton it was in what is known as Officers' Country.)

Like trying for about the fifteenth time, to learn to tat. My grandmother used to tat. Tatting, in case you don't know, is a form of lace making. Her tatting shuttle flew so fast sometimes it looked like a blur. Every time I try it I wind up with a disgraceful snarl of thread. I hadn't tried to tat for three or four years now, so I thought I was cured of that particular bit of insanity until a few weeks ago, when I'd noticed a female FBI agent tatting in the witness room, asked her to teach me how, and got hooked all over again.

I didn't want to try to tat at Lori's bedside. I was too likely to start swearing. I'd better do something I really knew how to do.

Last year, of course, I was making baby things. (No, not for Cameron—I now have two daughters producing offspring.) You know, cute little sweaters and baby afghans, all of which look like the crocheted kite string instead of pretty pastel yarn by about the sixteenth time they have to be washed because the baby threw up on them.

So this year I was crocheting a Christmas tree, and what that had to do with sitting by Lori's bed I hadn't the faintest idea. At least not consciously. Presumably there was a connection somewhere in my subconscious. Obviously there wasn't the least chance of my managing to mail out any Christmas cards this year.

I was feeling sorry for myself, and Donna, and Hal, and especially Lori, which all things considered probably was crappy of me, because I should have been feeling sorry for Clara Huffman. When I entered the house, after a brief discussion outdoors with the first officer on the scene, she was sitting on her nice blue couch—some kind of smooth cloth printed with big bold flowers in subdued shades of blue—twisting a piece of Kleenex in her hand. She was wearing a russet mohair sweater and a wool skirt printed with autumn leaves, but no shoes. The tiny bare toes in the thick carpet made her look oddly childlike.

Firmly thrusting Lori out of my mind, I fetched water for Clara. Men don't always think of things like that, and a lot of crying leaves even the most grief-stricken person thirsty. I offered to bring her aspirin. I offered to call a relative for her, and she said there weren't any relatives. Not any to matter, anyway. "No children?" I asked.

She shook her head drearily.

I called her doctor's office, getting the number from a list by the wall phone in the kitchen, to be told by his receptionist that Clara had already called, saying her husband was dead, and he—the doctor—was now on his way, Eric also having been his patient. She asked me what Eric had died of. "Clara didn't explain," she said, "but she sounded so upset Doctor thought he ought to go on over. So what—?"

"I think I'd better let the doctor tell you," I said.

"Oh, well, of course," she said, "but don't you even have an idea?"

"The doctor will tell you later," I said. "I've got to go now."

And go I did, back to the living room. Now I was waiting—patiently, at least in theory—for her to sign the consent-to-search form, without which, thanks to recent court decisions, we couldn't even search a crime scene.

I hadn't been able to get to the body at all, not even when I first arrived. I'd stayed in the living room, trying to get something out of Clara Huffman. Well. Supposedly trying. Perhaps I wasn't really trying very hard, because my sympathetic human side had momentarily submerged my pragmatic cop side, and besides that I had, for the moment, stopped feeling sorry for myself because I wanted to go home and crochet.

Really, it would have been hard for anybody not to feel sympathetic. From what little the first officer on the scene had been able to get before Mrs. Huffman finished collapsing, she'd been at the hairdresser's getting ready for a dinner party they'd planned to attend that night. Her husband, Eric—that, as I may have said, was the victim—had left to play golf early in the morning, and was still gone when she left. (Play golf on Friday morning? the patrol officer had asked, and she'd said he was semi-retired.) When she returned home she didn't find him at first; the door to his computer room was closed, and she didn't have any reason to open it, because his car wasn't home.

She didn't have any reason to open the door until she slipped off her shoes in the bedroom to walk, in her stocking feet, to the kitchen. In the hall right outside the computer room she stepped in something that was oozing under the door. Something unpleasant.

Very, very unpleasant.

So, of course, she opened the door to see what it was.

She was sobbing, now, on the couch, the expensive hairdo she'd paid for only a few hours ago now a tangled blue-gray mop, the neat manicure she'd probably gotten as she sat under the dryer now almost invisible as she continued to twist the disintegrating Kleenex in her hands.

I was sitting beside her, on the overstuffed decorator couch in the tastefully conventional living room. I wasn't sure she had even noticed I was there, although she'd answered me several times, each time rather mechanically. Clearly there was no use in my trying to ask her anything now, so I observed my surroundings carefully.

That isn't just nosiness on my part. The way the house looks can tell quite a lot about the personality of the inhabitants of the house, and except in the case of totally random violence—which isn't nearly as common as many people think—the personality of the victim has quite a lot to do with the cause of the crime.

At a glance—even at a stare—I couldn't see any reason at all for violence to hit this house, at least not from what I had seen of it so far.

Clara Huffman looked at me and said, "What?"

As I hadn't said anything at all for two or three minutes, I was a little confused. "I'm sorry?"

"That piece of paper. You wanted me to sign..."

"Yes, if you'd..."

"What is it? Eric told me..." Her face twisted momentarily. "Eric told me never to sign anything without knowing what it means."

"It gives us the right to search for evidence in the house. If you don't sign it then we have to wait and get a search warrant, and that could cause us to lose a lot of time."

"Evidence. You mean clues?"

Clues is not my favorite word. It makes me think of Nancy Drew and the Hardy boys, who interested me when I was twelve but seem far less entrancing now. After all, I wouldn't appreciate any teenagers coming and telling me how to investigate crimes. Anyway, I've never met a criminal who leaves things like twisted candles lying around.

But I agreed, "Yes. Clues. Fingerprints, weapons, things like that."

And also to do things like photograph the body, which definitely wasn't going to leave this house until it was properly photographed. I didn't tell Mrs. Huffman that. I didn't want to, unless I had to.

And I wouldn't have to, because she picked up the pen that was lying on an end table beside a writing pad and signed her name. I signed mine as witness, excused myself, and quietly delivered the paper to Irene Loukas, who said, "Hallelujah," and snapped the strobe onto the side of the camera.

She was the only police department evidence technician on the scene today. We'd quit sending two to homicides, unless the situation seemed to demand more than one, because it had finally been decreed by the Powers That Be that our evidence technician and the medical examiner's investigator could work together instead of repeating each other's work and retracing each other's steps.

What this meant, in practice, was that Irene was taking pictures while Gil Sanchez from the ME's office was sitting on the floor doing a quick, and pretty expert, sketch. Andrew Habib—Deputy Medical Examiner Andrew Habib, that is—had already arrived and, since he didn't have to wait for the consent search, departed.

How much work did it take to pronounce this body dead?

How much of an autopsy—except Habib prefers the term *post-mortem,* as he insists *autopsy* means surgery on oneself—was it going to take to say that this was an ax murder?

The single glance I'd had, as I handed over the consent search, had made it quite clear to me that Eric Huffman was dead.

Leaving the room, I couldn't help glancing surreptitiously at my watch. Five-thirty. Five-thirty, and I was supposed to have been at the hospital by five to spell Donna, who had to be on duty by six.

But Lori wouldn't notice whether Donna was there, or I was there, or Hal was there. Lori was asleep. As she had been for thirteen days now.

Feeling like weeping, I went back into the living room, wishing that either the doctor or another

policewoman would show up so that I could get on
to my real job, which was not holding hands with
the victim's spouse but rather asking questions. Because if I could get on to my real job, eventually I
could get through with it and go home and take care
of my husband and baby and then go to the hospital.

Clara had stopped crying. Maybe I could ask a
question or two with at least a slight hope of getting answers.

"Do you feel like talking with me now?" I asked.

She sniffed again and nodded.

Actually, I realized, she was bearing up magnifi-
cently. I didn't even want to think about how I'd
react if I arrived home to find... No. I wasn't even
going to think of Harry in that sort of condition.

"You said your husband was semi-retired," I
said. "What kind of work was he in?"

"He was an attorney."

That was a little bit of a surprise, in view of the
fact that I'd never heard of him. But then, on the
other hand, not all attorneys are in criminal law.

"What kind of practice?"

"Corporate."

"Never any criminal law?" I asked. "Or domestic cases?" I was thinking, what kind of person
would come into contact with an ax murderer? Not
even many criminals—that's the kind of violence
that usually turns up only in domestic situations.

She shook her head. "He wrote contracts, handled small corporate mergers, that kind of thing."

"Any, uh, unhappy clients that you know of?"

She shook her head again. "No. And I'd know."

"His files . . ."

She gestured toward the room he'd died in. "In there. I helped keep track of them. I typed up a lot of his work, until he got that computer and started doing it himself, and that was recently. He hadn't had anything at all big recently. If anybody was pissed I'd know."

Pissed. That was a word I'd use. It didn't seem to me to be the kind of word Clara Huffman—the kind of person Clara Huffman appeared to be—would use.

And I couldn't, in common humanity, ask her to go look through those files now and see if anything was missing.

"Was there any possible reason that you can think of?"

She might have answered me then. But I never will know for sure, because we were interrupted.

One of the patrolmen we'd left guarding the perimeter—this one was fairly new, a black man who looked about seven feet tall, though probably that was just because he was so thin; he probably wasn't really much over six-nine—opened the front door, looking apologetic. "Ms. Ralston, there's a Dr. Smiley here, says Ms. Huffman called him."

"Yes, let him in." I carefully did not smile at the *Ms*. Texans and other Southerners had always combined *Miss* and *Mrs*. into that slurred catchall pronounced *Miz*. In that respect, if no other, they had been way ahead of their time. I glanced at the officer's name tag—Kendall. I'd know him next time.

On seeing her doctor, Clara Huffman promptly burst into a fresh torrent of weeping, and I put the box of Kleenex on her lap.

Dr. Smiley, perhaps surprisingly (although probably I was stereotyping again, on the basis of other doctors I'd met at homocides), was not the hand-patting kind of doctor. His pleasantly rugged middle-aged face was calm and sympathetic, but not what my grandmother would have called goopy. He glanced at me first. "You a detective?" he asked.

"Yes," I said, rather pleased that he hadn't—as people usually do—informed me that I don't look like a detective.

"I thought you might be. You have the look about you." I tried to decide whether that was a compliment or not, as he pulled up a hassock and sat down in front of Mrs. Huffman. "Stop that," he said, very calmly. "It's all right to cry, but making yourself sick won't solve anything."

"Eric's *dead*," she wailed.

"I understand that."

"No, you don't understand! Somebody *murdered* him. They...they...you don't..."

He glanced at me, and I pointed toward the hall and then moved quietly in that direction. He said, "Will you excuse me just a minute?" and followed me.

"You'd better have a look," I said, and led him to the room.

Huffman's body was still there. I didn't even want to think about the task that whoever collected the body was going to have.

Smiley swallowed hard. "I haven't seen anything like that in a long time."

"You mean you *have* seen . . . ?"

He looked at me, nodded. "I saw a lot of things in 'Nam. Things I'd just as soon forget."

Harry has told me that, too.

"Yes, I've seen something like that before. I've seen things worse than that. But not lately. And God knows *she* hasn't. I think I'd better get her on to a hospital before she starts into shock. If she hasn't started already." He glanced back toward the living room.

"You want us to get an ambulance?"

"No, I'll go on and transport."

"Doctors don't usually—"

"Transport. Or make house calls, this day and age. But patients don't usually walk into something like this. And she's not as strong as she looks."

"She's taking it pretty well."

"Maybe too well," he said. "I'd rather treat for shock now than have to admit her to a psychiatric ward tomorrow. You need anything else from her?"

"No," I said. "What hospital?"

"Glenview, for now. I'll let you know if I have to move her. Uh...what's your name?"

"Deb Ralston," I said, and went back into the living room to locate my handbag and dig out my business card to give him. He glanced at it, stuck it in his billfold, and said, "Clara, I think we'd better get you on out of here."

"But Eric..." she began to protest.

"The police will take care of everything here," he said firmly. "You need to take care of yourself now. Why don't you get your shoes and bag, and let's go on out to my car."

"I can't get my bag," she said.

"Why can't you?"

"I dropped it. In there."

"In there?" I asked involuntarily. From what she'd told the patrolman, she'd gone to her bedroom, taken her shoes off, and was walking to the kitchen when she found the body. She was walking to the kitchen without her shoes and still carrying her handbag? That didn't make sense.

"I came in the house and the door to the study was open," she said. "And I went in to talk to Eric and I saw what was there and I dropped my handbag. Then...then I couldn't believe it was really true. It couldn't be true. Things like that happen to other people. Not to us. Not to our kind of people. So of course it wasn't real. I knew it couldn't be real. I was...I was seeing things. Things that weren't there. So I left and shut the door, so I wouldn't see things that weren't there. And I went in my bedroom and took my shoes off and I was going to go in the kitchen and get some orange juice and then I was going to go tell Eric what...what I thought...what I thought I saw, and Eric was going to laugh at me and tell me I better get my vision checked or get some new glasses or something. And then I was walking down the hall without my shoes and I...stepped in...in some...sticky stuff. Sticky red stuff. And I looked on my feet and there was blood on my feet and then...then...then I knew it was real. It really was real and I couldn't go tell Eric because it was real and it really happened...really happened... But I forgot. When I was talking to that black man I forgot I went in there before. I didn't remember until just now, when you said get my bag and then I...remembered...where my bag is, and..."

"I'll get your bag," I said.

"No! I can't... You don't understand! It's in *there!* I don't want—"

"What if I just get your billfold? Will that be okay? Since it's inside your bag nothing could have gotten on it."

"My billfold? Yes. I guess that's okay. Yes, you can..."

The billfold was a deep maroon leather French purse, and I checked to be sure it contained identification, insurance cards, checkbook, as well as cash. No cigarettes in the purse, so probably she didn't smoke. What else would she need?

What does a woman need to take to the hospital with her, if she's going to the hospital to be treated for shock because her husband has just been murdered in a particularly nasty way?

I didn't know.

I just took her billfold. That, and a pair of Grasshoppers I found in the bedroom closet a good ten feet from where she'd peeled off the blood-stained pantyhose and left the brown dress pumps.

She didn't seem even to see it, and Dr. Smiley took it out of my hand. "Come on, Clara," he said, "let's get you on into the hospital."

She resisted, then. "I want to see Eric."

I didn't hear what the doctor said then, because Irene beckoned to me from the hall and I got up and went that direction. "She was lying," Irene said to me.

"About what?"

"About saying she didn't go in there until she had her shoes off."

"I know..." I began.

But Irene wasn't listening to me; she was gesturing with the spray can of luminol in her hand.

I had better explain about luminol.

Most blood marks are visible. Usually, at this type of crime scene, very visible. But some traces of blood, especially if somebody has made an attempt to wash them out, are a lot harder to see. In that case, you spray luminol wherever you think blood might be. Then you turn on a black light, and the invisible blood marks become clearly visible.

"The marks leading out of the scene were patent," Irene said. (That's *patent* with a long *a*—at least it has a long *a* the way most police say it— meaning visible, the opposite of *latent,* meaning invisible and yet to be developed. It's a term usually used in relation to fingerprints, but it's perfectly correct in this usage also.) "So I just followed and started spraying where I lost the trail. It led to this bedroom. And these brown dress shoes. So she was in there in her shoes and then again, later, without them, because the second trail led to those stockings like she said, and then to that telephone in her bedroom. So I guess that's where she called from. Then she went in that bathroom and washed her feet. I've got the washcloth and towel. So she was lying when she said she just—"

"Irene—" I tried to interrupt.

"So if she was lying about that you'd better find out—"

"Irene—" I said for the second or third time.

This time she heard me.

"What?"

"I already know she was in there in her shoes. She just told her doctor and me both. She'd blanked it out earlier."

"Yeah?" Irene's disbelief was as patent as the beginning of the blood trail.

"People do that," I said more or less patiently. "Get confused, I mean. It happens all the time. It's shock. Anyway, there's nothing suspicious about it."

"If she lied—"

"Irene," I pointed out, "if anybody could wreak that carnage in there and not get blood anywhere but on his or her shoes, I'd really like to meet that person."

Irene turned slowly, looking back in the direction of the room still containing the body. "Oh," she said, "yeah." She shrugged. "Guess I better leave the detecting to you, huh?"

That left me with nothing to say, because the fact is Irene is probably the best ident tech in Texas. She just tends to let her imagination run away with her a little too much to be good in the detective department. But who am I to judge? I let my imagination run away all too often myself.

"Let me check on her again," I said. But the living room was now empty. Apparently the doctor had managed to talk Clara out to the car. "You can show me the scene now," I said to Irene. "I didn't get much of a chance to look at it earlier."

"Busy babysitting?"

"Yeah. Busy babysitting."

Irene led me back to the bedroom that had served as a computer room, and I looked around carefully. In terms of overall quantity of litter it wasn't quite the messiest crime scene I had ever set eyes upon. The problem was in just what that litter consisted of. It was a shambles—and that was a word I had used for probably thirty years before I found out what it really means. A *shambles* was an old-fashioned slaughterhouse. Before sanitation, before easy cleaning, a shambles was undoubtedly a horrifying sight, a horrifying smell.

I had quit using the term when I found out that it didn't mean the general chaos and messiness I'd always assumed.

It was the only possible word now. The room was a shambles. But even so, there were some unusual things. I mean, the FBI has made a careful study of what different things a crime scene indicate. For example, and this one is practically the classic, if a pet is killed as well as members of a family, almost always the murderer is a member of the family, because to an outsider the pet is a thing and to a family member the pet is a member of the family. Unfortunately, that particular discovery has been so widely publicized that too many people know it. And now we find pets killed by outsiders who want the police to *think* it was an insider killing.

But to the best of my knowledge, even the FBI hasn't gotten into the matter of what it means when somebody kills a computer as well as a person.

That sounds like I'm trying to be funny. I'm not. The situation was anything but funny. Whoever took the ax—or machete or whatever it was, but I was guessing an ax and so was Dr. Habib—to Eric Huffman had used the same instrument on other contents of the room, and it was now only by means of a reasonable familiarity with computers that I was able to tell that those broken chunks of metal and plastic had once been an expensive and well-designed computer system.

"Get out of my way," Gil Sanchez said in a tone friendlier than his words, and I began to get out of his way. He was in the process of collecting evidence, and it was evidence I wanted as little as possible to do with. This, I decided, would be a good time for me to do a complete walk-through of the house.

Dutch had probably done that already, but I hadn't the slightest idea where Dutch was. Probably out talking with neighbors, as I hadn't seen him since about two minutes after we arrived.

Anyway, I didn't make the walk-through yet, because as I was moving to get out of Gil's way I saw something, and I had picked it up before I even thought not to.

"Did I say you could touch that?" Irene yelled.

"Oh, come off it, Irene," I said, exhibiting my find, several pages of computer printout that had clearly been wadded up and stuck in the trash can before the trash can had been upended on the floor. "What in the world makes you think X would have touched this?"

"How do you know the killer *didn't* touch it?" Irene retorted. But then she shrugged. "You've got it, you might as well keep it."

I escaped with the printout, three pages of complete gibberish, which I spread out on the kitchen table.

I say complete gibberish. Actually it wasn't. And the reason I knew it wasn't was because you could find identical printouts in my own house, in the trash can beside Harry's computer. That is, you could find it in the trash can after I picked it up and stuffed it into the trash can, because Harry had been too cross to do it.

There are networks, or nets, that computer people belong to, or pay to use. There are viruses that get into computers. The viruses are often spread over the computer nets via modems. Several weeks ago such a virus had taken up residence in Harry's computer. There had been much screaming, yelling, cursing, and swearing on Harry's part when he couldn't print out the papers for the MBA he is working on, especially when he took the disks up to Kinko's to try to get them printed there and Kinko's—quite reasonably in my opinion—wouldn't let him load the disks onto their computers.

Eventually he managed to get rid of the virus, with a vaccination program he had loaded from the same net. But that was only after several days of complete frustration.

The virus was an interesting one, according to Harry, who has fallen in love with computers. According to Harry, there was nothing visibly wrong on the monitor. That is, everything on the monitor looked completely normal. But whenever the user tried to print, every letter came out wrong. Every letter was represented by the one immediately before it in the alphabet except, of course, for A, which was represented by Z. Thus *Harry Ralston* came out *Gzqqx Qzkrsnm*. Kind of cute, when you're reading it in a Xanth novel—that's fantasy by Piers Anthony, which I started reading when Hal left them lying around the house when I was home right after Cameron was born. I wound up buying some for myself, because they're wonderfully full of puns and make great escape reading. Anthony does not explain the code, but sooner or later—more later than sooner, if the reader is me—the reader figures it out. It occurs when a resident of Xanth, which is a magical version of the Florida peninsula, is trying to talk to a Mundanian, who is a resident of the Real World. When the Mundanian is trying to talk to the Xanthian, each letter is represented by the letter after it in the alphabet. Or maybe it's the other way around. I forget.

Kind of cute, when it's meant for fun. But very, very frustrating when it turns up in business letters or classwork.

And although it's a simple substitution code, there was at least a chance that whoever created the virus was, like me, a reader of Xanth novels.

Either the virus was circulating other ways also, or else Eric Huffman had belonged to the same computer users' network Harry belonged to.

Which, I supposed, meant absolutely nothing, since according to Harry several thousand people used that particular network.

Anyway, I reasoned, once I translated all this into English I might know what Eric had been working on during his last day of life. That was a guess, of course, since Harry's computer's attack of virus had been several weeks ago, but I suspected that the trash might get emptied in this house more often than in mine. If so, then Eric—unlike Harry—hadn't managed to cure the virus yet.

Leaving the printout on the kitchen table for Irene to collect as evidence, I departed on my delayed tour of the house. The first thing I noticed—well, one of the first things; I actually spotted it when I was hunting Clara's shoes—was that they had separate bedrooms. Which might, or might not, mean anything at all. A need for sleep—maybe he snores and she crawls around in the bed in her sleep—doesn't prove lack of affection. Some couples visit each other's bedrooms but retire to their own for sleeping purposes. What I'm saying is that I didn't want to read into the separate bedrooms more than was there.

The third bedroom was Eric Huffman's computer room, and the fourth seemed to be a guest room. The pink bedspread had only a bare mattress below it, and the closet was empty except for several evening gowns zipped into a plastic bag.

Dining room. Table and buffet and china cabinet. Attractively unimaginative china. Attractively unimaginative silver (and in the unlikely event that X was a burglar caught in the act, wouldn't he have taken the silver?). A breakfast room separated from the kitchen by a breakfast bar. A den; that was where the TV and a big fireplace were, and some books and some magazines. A lot of books and magazines, I corrected myself. One of them, at least, was a reader.

Probably both, because the subjects were pretty widely varying.

Off the den, a mudroom/laundry combination, washer and dryer. No ironing board. Probably, like most of the rest of us, she'd either thrown out everything but permanent-press clothes, or sent anything needing ironing to the cleaners.

Through the laundry, the door into the garage.

And there was a little surprise. A cot with bedding on it.

If there was a guest, why wasn't the guest sleeping in the guest room?

If there wasn't a guest, who'd been sleeping in the garage?

A servant? But she hadn't mentioned a servant to me. Maybe she forgot, but that was something you'd think she'd certainly remember.

Anyway, there wasn't enough stuff here for a live-in servant, and why would a servant that wasn't live-in need a cot?

"Ms. Ralston?"

I raised the garage door, that being the easiest way to get out to where Kendall was calling me. "I'm over here," I called. "By the way, people usually just call me Deb."

"Ms. Ralston, I mean Deb, I caught this guy prowling around outside. He says he lives here."

He was blond, husky, maybe about nineteen. Blue eyes, fair skin, clean-shaven, fairly short hair. He had that frank, open face that so often hides the con man. "Who are you?" I asked.

"Shane Corbett," he said. "I live here. That's my bed right there."

He was pointing toward the cot.

"What're all the police doing here?" he asked belatedly.

"Shane Corbett," I said, "I want to have a talk with you."

"Yeah?" he said. "Who're you?"

Mentally I sighed. Obviously it was going to take me a lot longer to get home than I had planned, even at the worst.

TWO

BY THE TIME I had finished explaining to the satisfaction—I should say to the wide-eyed delight—of Shane Corbett exactly who and what I was, Dutch had returned from wherever it was that he had gone, and we had to go through the whole rigamarole of explanations again so Shane would know who Dutch was. These explanations were frequently interrupted—by Shane, of course—with exclamations such as "Wow!" and "Far out!" (which expression I had thought was decently buried a decade ago), though there was a considerable sprinkling of "Cool!" and "Ba-a-ad!"

"But what are the cops doing here?" he demanded for the fifth time.

Watching his reaction, I said, "Because somebody murdered Mr. Huffman."

His mouth snapped shut for a moment. He was, at the very least, startled, though I couldn't guess for sure whether his expression represented real grief or just the fear that he might now find himself short of a place to live. Then he said, "Shiiit." He paused. Then he asked, *"Mr.* Huffman? Why him?"

"I thought maybe you could tell me."

He shook his head. "If it was her—but I don't know why anybody'd want to hurt him. I really don't. He— Damn. Damn." Genuine grief, I guessed now. But on one like Shane, all emotions would be shallow, and it didn't take him long to start chattering again, about how this was just like cop shows on television and he'd always wondered if real life worked like cop shows.

We still hadn't gotten into any questions, and I was beginning to feel exactly the way I feel when I am trying to get sense out of my scatterbrained seventeen-year-old son Hal.

"So Shane Corbett is your full name?" I finally managed to ask.

"Yeah. Well, Shane Dennis Corbett, but nobody ever calls me Dennis. Hey, how come you're writing that down?"

"I always write everything down."

"How come?"

"So I won't forget what people say."

"Oh. Yeah, I guess that makes sense." He wriggled a little and crossed his hands in front of him on the kitchen table, that being where we were sitting, and looked at me with that air of bright expectancy that, in Hal, usually means he's going to hear at least half of what I say and misunderstand no more than about a fourth of it.

Actually there was no physical resemblance at all between the two. Hal, whom we adopted when he was just a few months old, is half Korean. The Koreans are usually a short people, but we are forced to assume the other half, the non-Korean, was very, very tall, as Hal seems—we devoutly hope—to have topped out at six foot five. He's got sort of darkish yellowish coloring, eyes that are so brown they are almost black, and straight black hair. Shane, at the most about five-eight, had blond hair that almost wanted to be gold, and the most limpid blue eyes I'd seen in a long time. But the *feel* of the two—and I hope you know what I mean by that—was just about identical.

He was still looking at me brightly. Deliberately brightly, so that I would notice he was being attentive.

"So you live here," I said.

"Yeah."

"How long?"

"How long what?"

I had guessed right. His brain was wired the same way as Hal's. "How long have you lived here?"

"Oh. I thought that might be what you meant, but then I thought you might mean how long was I gonna live here."

"Shane..." My voice was rising slightly, as my eyes involuntarily caught sight of the kitchen clock.

"Six weeks," he said hastily.

"Where'd you live before that?"

"Well, I didn't exactly..." He glanced nervously at Dutch, who was towering over him with a face

like a thundercloud, and said, "I mean...well...
sometimes I lived at the Salvation Army Men's
Shelter, and sometimes, well you know..."

Dutch cleared his throat.

"Trinity Park," Shane said. "If you like, you
know, pick your spot right, like under a picnic table or something, you're out of the rain most of the
time and the cop cars can't see you very well when
they come through with their lights and all. For a
while I was in Galveston, but you know, down there
there's not much place to sleep 'cept right on the
beach and the cops there, you know, they don't like
people to sleep on the beach and they drive along the
beach in these, like, station wagon things and hassle people if they're sleeping there or sometimes they
arrest them, so I came back to Fort Worth, and
Trinity Park, see. It's a real nice place, only it got
kinda cold, you know, and so I went to the Men's
Shelter, only they had all these, like, rules and stuff,
and I had to work at their workshop and I wanted
to, you know, find a better job, so I was walking
around downtown and, um, I saw this guy going to
the library and he looked like a nice guy..."

Translated, he looked like an easy touch, I
thought, as Shane paused for breath.

"...so I asked this guy, you know, if he had any,
like, work I could do and he said no but we talked a
while and he said I could, like, stay with him awhile

until I got a job and a place of my own that I could afford."

"So who was this guy?" Dutch demanded.

Shane looked at him. "Well, Eric, of course. I mean who else... Look, he was a real nice guy. This here killing, this just don't make sense! I mean, who'd want to kill Eric? Now if it was Mrs. Huffman..." His voice trailed off.

"Tell me about Mrs. Huffman," Dutch said, his voice now very soft.

"What do you want me to say? I mean, you met her, didn't you?"

"I didn't," Dutch said.

"I talked with her," I said, "but if you've been living with her..."

An unfortunate choice of words, apparently, because Shane snickered a little before answering. "Not with her. I lived here, but not with her. I mean, look, he's...he was...a real nice guy. I mean, for an old guy, he was..." Shane paused, apparently hunting an adjective other than nice, old, cool, or ba-a-ad, none of which seemed to fit. I could see him surrender; the struggle was too great. "He was okay. He was real nice. But her!"

"You have been talking for five friggin' minutes," Dutch said not quite accurately, "and you haven't said one friggin' word that's worth anything. To sum up: You're a vagrant. Eric Huffman took you in. You don't like his wife. And that's all you've said. Now. Why don't you like her?''

''She doesn't like me. I don't not like her.''

''Why doesn't she like you?''

''She said I had lice.''

''Did you?'' I inquired.

''Yeah, but it wasn't my fault. I mean, they're like colds. You catch 'em. It wasn't like I did it apurpose.''

That, of course, was perfectly true; any school-teacher knows that lice have no respect for socioeconomic class.

''Okay,'' Dutch said, semi-patiently, ''if she said you had lice and you had lice, what—''

''Well, Eric, just got me some shampoo stuff, you know, but she said I couldn't sleep in the guest room, so she and Eric had this big fight about it and then Eric said I could use this cot out here in the garage . . . I mean it's not bad, the garage is, like, you know, heated and all that, but it's kinda silly to have to sleep out here when there's a perfectly good room . . . and I don't have lice anymore, I mean, I washed my hair and all my clothes and stuff and my head doesn't itch anymore so I know I don't have 'em anymore, but she still wouldn't let me in the house, I mean, I could go in to eat and watch TV and like, you know, pee and all that, but I couldn't sleep in the house.''

I couldn't see that all this was getting us any-where. Shane's dislike for Clara Huffman was immaterial. It wasn't she who was killed. And given that he was a scatterbrained vagrant who had suddenly been dumped on her, complete with lice, her perfectly understandable insistence that he sleep in the garage said nothing, so far as I could see, about her character. And her character was not in question anyway, except for the simple fact that when a person is killed in a domestic setting we—the police—automatically look first at the spouse.

"Deb, I want to talk to you," Dutch said. "Corbett, you stay right here, you hear me?"

"Yes, sir."

I followed Dutch into the living room, where he cornered me on the far side of the piano to demand, "Did you give him a Miranda?"

"No, but—"

"Then what in the hell are we doing talking to him?"

"Dutch, he's not a suspect," I protested.

"If he's not a suspect then what in the bloody hell do you call him?"

"Dutch, for cryin' out loud—"

"He was here—"

"He lives here. That doesn't mean he was actually here in the house when—"

"He was here," Dutch repeated, "or at least he could have been here. And what do you bet he's got a record?"

"Of course he's got a record," I agreed. "Probably vagrancy, maybe public intox, maybe theft, something like that. But it's a far cry from public intox to—"

"Opportunity," Dutch interrupted, counting on his fingers. "Weapon—there's a fireplace, there's wood, that means there's damn well got to be an ax—"

"Not necessarily," I interrupted. "They could have bought the wood already chopped."

"They'd still have an ax," Dutch argued. "This kind of people, they'd have one for show if nothing else. I'm telling you, the kid had—"

"Opportunity and weapon, sure," I agreed, "but what on earth kind of motive could he have had? Huffman had taken him in, was sheltering him, feeding him—"

"How much cash did Huffman have on hand?" Dutch asked. "Where was Corbett before he went to Galveston? Where—"

"He said he 'came back' to Fort Worth," I interrupted, "so—"

"So at one point he was in Fort Worth. That doesn't mean that's where he was most recently before Galveston. Or where he was before that, or before that. Or where he wanted to go next. You know that kind of person never stays put long. Where did he plan to go next? How far could he go on whatever cash Huffman had on him? Deb, we don't have to prove motive."

"I fully realize that. But I'd still like to see one. If he killed Huffman for the money to get to his next destination, then why is he here now? Why isn't he already on the road?"

"Damned if I know," Dutch said. "Maybe he's too dumb to realize we'd suspect him. Maybe he came back to get his clothes or the car or some jewelry or something. Or maybe I'm barking up the wrong tree. But if you don't give him his rights I'm going to, and I think it'd come better from you."

"What makes you think that?"

"This is the wrong time to scare him," Dutch said. "At least not much. If we can scare him a little, just enough to get him coherent, that's one thing, but I don't want to spook him into clamming up. And I damn sure don't want to blow this case by not giving him his rights if he does turn out to be the one."

"Dutch, I realize all that. But I just don't consider him a suspect."

"Well, I do. If you don't think it's him, who do you suspect? Her?" His tone of voice said plainly how silly that idea was.

"No," I admitted, "not her." Clara Huffman, if I remembered correctly was at least two inches shorter than my five-two, twenty to thirty pounds lighter than my hundred and twenty. I could not, even with my vivid imagination, conjure up a mental picture of her taking an ax to Eric Huffman, who'd been—as best I could tell from the remains—over six feet and around two hundred pounds. Even if she did have a reason, which I had no reason at all to suspect, she was physically incapable of it. "Dutch," I said, "I don't have a suspect. But we're less than two hours into this investigation. It's really too early to think about a suspect, unless one falls into our lap."

"I'm not saying I'm ready to make a case on Corbett," Dutch agreed. "I'm just saying let's be sure our asses are covered if we do decide, down the road—"

"Oh, all right," I said crossly. I couldn't, after all, explain to Dutch that I refused to suspect Shane Corbett of murder because he felt, in some way I was totally incapable of defining, like my son.

I preceded Dutch back into the kitchen. Shane had semi-obeyed. He was still in the kitchen, but he was now eating a peanut butter and jelly sandwich and drinking a glass of milk. A carton of milk, a loaf of bread, a jar of jelly, a jar of peanut butter, an iced-tea spoon, two knives, and a trail of crumbs littered the previously pristine white Formica countertop. "Shane," I said, exactly as I would have said it to Hal, "didn't you forget something?"

"Huh?" He turned around in his chair, looked at the countertop. "Oh," he said. "Well. Yeah."

Dutch watched, in barely concealed astonishment at the interruption, while Shane cleaned the counter, restored the peanut butter to the pantry, the jelly and milk to the refrigerator, and the bread to the bread box, dropped the knives and spoon into the sink, and dusted the crumbs into his hand before dumping them into the garbage disposal.

"I always forget things like that," Shane said. He sat down and took another bite of the sandwich.

"Shane," I said, "when we're talking to people at the scene of a crime, if there's even the least little bitty chance that they might've been the one to commit the crime, then the courts have ruled that we've got to tell them about their rights."

"Oh, you mean like on television?" He was talking around the peanut butter. "You mean like, 'You have the right to remain silent,' and all that?"

"Yeah, like that," I said, and went on through the spiel. Slowly, he laid the sandwich down on the table.

"Yeah, but I didn't kill anybody," he objected. "So why're you telling me that stuff?"

"Just in case you did," Dutch said.

"Are you going to arrest me?"

"Is there any reason we should?" I asked.

"No, but you're telling me all that stuff."

"Usually we tell anybody who shows up at the scene of an unwitnessed crime about their rights," I said.

"Have I got to sign that piece of paper?"

"No," I said, "and if you don't sign it then I can't ask you any more questions."

"And then," Dutch added, "we get to wonder why you don't want to answer questions." He was standing, one foot on a kitchen chair, looming over

Shane in a manner that just barely avoided being threatening.

The statement and posture, I suppose I need not say, are not official portions of the Miranda warning. They are, however, very often tacked on at the end.

"Well," Shane said, "I don't mind answering questions. I guess. Not really." But he continued to gaze doubtfully at the consent form.

"You can always change your mind, if I start asking questions you don't like," I said. He shrugged and scrawled his name, and Dutch grabbed the form and added his signature as witness.

"I never did get your date of birth," I said. He gave it to me. If he was telling the truth, he was now twenty-two, which was a little bit of a surprise. I'd have placed him as no more than nineteen, tops. I got his Social Security number—a Texas prefix, which didn't particularly surprise me—and then asked for his driver's license.

"I don't have one," he said. "See, they won't let me have a driver's license unless I took driver's ed, or unless I already have one from another state, and I, uh, dropped out of high school before I got around to driver's ed, and I haven't got the money to take one of those, you know, courses from Sears and like that, and every state I go to wants me to take driver's ed. Somebody told me you don't have to take driver's ed in Wyoming. You s'pose that's true?"

"I haven't the faintest idea," I said. "Shane—"

"Maybe I ought to go there and find out," he said enthusiastically.

"You're not going anywhere right now," Dutch informed him.

"But I've got to—"

"Try it and see how fast you get into jail."

"But I've got to go somewhere!"

"What makes you think—"

Shane interrupted him. "You don't think she's gonna let me stay here, do you? Not with Eric dead she's not. She'll chase me out of here so fast my head'll be spinning. Oh, well," he added despondently, "I guess I can go back to the Salvation Army. It's too cold to sleep in the park. Only they have so many rules there."

I had this horrible feeling in my stomach that told me I'd already decided what to do before the thought made its way into my conscious mind. I didn't like it at all, but I was going to do it anyway. That was perfectly clear.

"Excuse me a minute," I said, and went to the phone to call Harry.

The only real question, of course, was how Hal would take it. Normally Hal would have been delighted. But this wasn't normally.

WITH THE PROMISE of a place to live—with a *cop*, no less, and a lady cop at that, which Shane apparently regarded as adding a certain cachet to the situation—he'd cheered up a lot, and was now talking and gesturing expansively. Dutch, with the kitchen chair propped on its back legs sort of leaning against the refrigerator (in a position I'd never let Hal get in since the time he tipped the chair all the way over, to land on his back with the breath knocked out of him and the chair irreparable), was listening intently, and I was making occasional notes.

"So he'd had a, like, you know, heart attack or stroke or something like that, I forget what and of course I wasn't here when it happened, but he'd sort of retired because he couldn't... I mean, he wasn't s'posed to get too excited or anything like that anymore, and he didn't go to work anymore except sometimes, I mean, he was real nice and he let me use his car—" Shane came to a dead stop.

"Without a driver's license," Dutch drawled.

"Well...uh...he didn't exactly ask me if I had a driver's license."

"And you didn't exactly tell him."

"No. I mean, look, man, I can drive just fine. I just don't have a—"

"License," Dutch supplied drily.

"Yeah." His overall attitude at the moment was somewhere between defensive and cocky.

"So he let you use his car to go where?"

"Well, to go job hunting. And a couple of times I got jobs and he said I could use his car to go to work only, well, I don't know why, the jobs never seemed to last too long. Like one time I got this job doing framing, you know what that is? Construction, like?"

"Yeah. It's the first part of putting up the walls," Dutch said.

"Okay, so I got this job framing. And I told him I'd worked in framing before, and I had, down in Florida. But they said, after a couple of days they said I was doing it all wrong and so they fired me."

"How long had you worked in framing in Florida?" I asked.

"Well, a couple of days. They fired me too. I mean, look, how'm I gonna learn if everybody keeps firing me?"

"Danged if I know," Dutch said. "Okay, let me be sure we've got this straight. Huffman used to lend you his car to go job hunting and to go to work. You got a job doing framing but it only lasted a couple of days. That right?"

"Yes, sir."

"Not much framing going on in November and December," Dutch said.

"Well, yeah, that was in September."

"This is December."

"So?"

"You said you've just lived here six weeks," I pointed out. "Now you're saying you were borrowing Eric Huffman's car as early as September."

"Oh. Well, yeah, I guess it must've been more than six weeks, then."

"It wasn't too cold to sleep outside in September," Dutch pointed out.

"But—"

"When did you get up here from Galveston?"

"I don't remember. July, August, sometime like that. It was after the Fourth of July, anyway. Man, those fireworks on the seawall were *something else.*"

"And then you were living in Trinity Park."

"Yeah."

"And then you went to the Salvation Army."

"Yeah."

"When was that?"

"I don't exactly remember."

"But you went there because it was too cold to sleep in the park." Dutch was firing questions fast now, and I had become a passive observer.

"Yeah."

"But you don't remember when that was."

"Uh-uh."

"S'pose they'll have records that'll tell me?"

"I don't know. They might."

"But it was before September."

"I don't remember if it was before September or not."

"But you were working in construction in September and getting there driving Eric Huffman's car."

"Maybe it was October."

"Maybe what was October?"

"When I was working in construction. I know I got the job real soon after I came to live here."

The questions went on like that for another half hour, during which time we were able to establish that Shane had worked for two or three restaurants, a yard service, and the city zoo, all for periods of no longer than a week, during the time he'd lived with the Huffmans. To Dutch, of course, it looked suspicious. Shane Corbett couldn't keep his dates straight, his times straight. To me, used to Hal's insanities, it didn't look suspicious.

Well, not very suspicious.

Dutch finally got tired of asking questions and sent Shane out to the garage to pack up his possessions. Then, doing a visible double take, he headed into the garage to watch Shane pack up his possessions.

I went to take my first really complete walk-through of the house. The body was finally being packed up, though the task of getting it into a body bag was taking somewhat longer than such a task normally takes. Irene was packing up her kits, and the rest of the medical examiner's team had already departed. "Irene," I asked, "where's the ax?"

"I wish I knew," she replied.

"You mean you didn't find it?"

"I mean we didn't find it. For all I know it might have been a machete or something, except Habib says it was an ax."

"Did you look outside?" I asked, a split second before realizing Irene would—probably correctly—regard such a question as an insult.

"Of course I looked outside," she said. "I looked outside. I looked inside. I looked upstairs and downstairs and in my lady's chamber, except there isn't an upstairs or a downstairs. I looked in the cars, both of 'em. I looked in the toolshed. I looked in the garage. I looked behind the books in the bookshelves. I looked in the freezer. I looked in the garbage cans. I looked every damn place you can think of and some you can't. I even walked to the corner and looked down the storm sewer. There is not an ax anywhere around here. Or a hatchet. Or a machete. Or a meat cleaver. Or any other cutting instrument larger than a butcher knife, and if you think a butcher knife did that damage then you've got a heck of a lot better imagination than I have."

"I wasn't trying to pick a fight," I said.

"Well, it sure sounded like you were. You know I always find everything there is to find. I found that paint chip in that girl's clothes, didn't I?"

That girl was Lori. That gray paint chip from the sweatsuit she'd worn to the library that night could have come from any gray Ford, Lincoln, or Mercury manufactured in the last three years. It wasn't exactly a glorious clue, but it was all we had.

I agreed that Irene had found that chip of paint, and Irene looked a little more cheerful. "Look, I'm going to come back out here tomorrow morning and search all over again. You want to come with me?"

I didn't and she knew I didn't. But I'd just done a good job of painting myself into a corner. "You can do it just fine by yourself," I said, watching her preen, "but I suppose if I come along too—"

"Right. And if you don't I'll have to bring Bob or Sarah." She was quite correct. No police officer with sense enough to come in out of the rain ever searches a crime scene alone. There should always be at least two people who can testify to any findings.

So it appeared that I was going to help search a crime scene tomorrow.

I went back into the kitchen. "I stuck him in the back of the car," Dutch said. "Deb, you sure you want to take him home with you, especially with you spending so much time up at the hospital and all?"

"Harry's at home all day," I pointed out.

"So was Eric Huffman."

He could have gone all day without saying that.

THREE

WHEN I FINALLY did get home, I found Harry sitting at his computer table doing something—I wouldn't care to venture a guess as to what—with an expression on his face like a thunderstorm. Hal was at the kitchen table, with several encyclopedia volumes spread out in front of him, writing furiously—and *furiously* is the operative word. If Harry looked like a thunderstorm, Hal more closely resembled the sky before a tornado.

Only Cameron seemed in a good mood, and that was doubtless because Harry had not yet noticed that Cameron had been eating the newest issue of *Soldier of Fortune* and Cameron had not yet noticed that the cat (the old cat, not the new cat) had once again chewed off the end of the nipple on his baby bottle—to no avail. The bottle at the moment contained cherry Kool-Aid. Cats do not drink Kool-Aid.

At twenty-one months, Cameron should not still want a bottle. But he doesn't read—or eat—the books that say so.

Hal glared at me and kept on writing. Harry glared at Hal and kept on doing whatever he was doing. Cameron, in a hurry to get to me, planted one foot firmly on the bottle, squirting even more Kool-Aid out onto the floor. I picked him up and set the bottle upright on the coffee table. The cat began stalking it, clearly in hopes that this time it contained something more delicious than Kool-Aid. "Hello," I said to my family, most of whom seemed to be ignoring me. "This is Shane. He's going to live with us for a while."

"In *my* room?" Hal demanded.

"Where would you suggest I put him?" I inquired. "On the roof?"

"He can use Cameron's room. There's two beds in there."

That was true, as Cameron's room used to be Vicky and Becky's room, until Vicky married a lawyer and moved out and Becky married a medical student (and financial whiz kid) and moved out.

"Okay," I said. "I just thought you might want to get to know him."

"All I *want* to do," Hal said, "is go to the *hospital,* but *he* won't let me till I finish this stupid *history* report and it's the stupid *weekend* for cryin' out loud and I can finish the report *later.* "

"That does sound fairly reasonable," I said cautiously. "When is the report due?"

"Monday," Hal said, with a quick glance at Harry.

"Last Monday," Harry said. "He also has two weeks' worth of geometry, a chemistry lab report,

and an English paper. He seems to be current in PE."

"I was gonna do them," Hal said. "But I was worried about Lori."

"The school called me today," Harry said. "The principal told me everybody's been as patient as possible, in view of the situation, but if his grades don't pick up he's in danger of not graduating."

"I was gonna do it," Hal yelled. "But right now I've got to go see *Lori!*"

"Hal," I said as gently as I could, "Lori doesn't know—"

"I *know* she doesn't!" he yelled. "But *I* do!"

Hal was right. So was Harry. Unfortunately, this was a case in which two "rights" were in head-on collision.

I showed Shane where he could put his things, changed Cameron, changed myself (due to the condition of Cameron's diaper when I picked him up), and went into the kitchen, still balancing Cameron on my hip, to see what I could think of for supper that required absolutely no thought and very little time or effort.

Finding nothing of interest in the fridge, I went on out to the garage to look in the freezer. Fish sticks. Frozen potato nuggets. Frozen mixed veggies (in the microwave, while the other stuff is in the oven). That nice refrigerator cole slaw I made several days ago, if somebody hadn't eaten it all.

Another look in the fridge told me nobody had eaten it. Good. There was supper.

I gave Cameron to Harry so that he (Cameron, I mean) couldn't get underfoot while I was cooking.

Shane wandered out into the kitchen and asked if he could help me. I'll admit that was a bit of a surprise, but I recovered well enough to suggest he set the table. That, of course, involved dislodging Hal, who stomped furiously off into his bedroom carrying the encyclopedia volumes, which belong in the garage, that being the only place we have with room for bookshelves. All this—the books, the washer, the dryer, the freezer, Hal's weight bench set, all Harry's retired or temporarily retired hobbies, the kitchen-y things I don't have room for in the kitchen (I have frequently expressed my opinion of that kitchen)—means that our allegedly two-car garage is in fact a no-car garage, which in turn means that our front yard looks like a parking lot or—considering the condition of the cars—a junkyard, complete with a pit bull as a junkyard dog to guard it.

Said pit bull was whining at the back door trying to get in to kiss the baby. I declined to admit him, but did check his food and water. Considering the mood everybody else was in, I wouldn't care to gamble that anybody had thought to feed either dog or cats.

We used to feed the dog on the patio and the cats on the kitchen floor, until I caught Cameron eating cat food. This was before he began eating dog food.

Then we fed the dog and the cats on the patio, until we caught the dog eating the cats' food despite the cats' fury. Now we feed the cats on the hood of the pickup truck, because neither the baby nor the dog can get up there. We don't have to worry about the baby eating the dog's food anymore because the dog wised up. Now he eats it before the baby can get there. The dog's water is sometimes a problem, but Cameron doesn't drink it; he only uses it for a fingerbowl. The cats' water bowl sits on the counter in the bathroom. On the back of the counter, that is.

I was rattling on about these things to an obviously amused Shane (who went and fed the cats, the dog having already been fed) because I didn't want to think. Didn't want to think about today's murder, didn't want to think about Lori's coma, or about the fact that Harry and Hal seemed extraordinarily mad at one another.

The conversation at supper was about what you'd expect. There wasn't any, unless you consider "Pass the salt" to be scintillating dialogue.

I left Shane to do the dishes—if he was going to live with me, he might as well expect chores—while I fed Cameron fruit yogurt to top off the fish sticks, potatoes, and peas he'd semi-eaten during the family dinner. Then I took Cameron for his bath. Theoretically he goes to bed at seven o'clock. Of course, as anybody with a baby knows, this is definitely only theoretical.

The way our house is laid out, the master bedroom with its own bath is in the back left corner of the house. In the front left, off the living room and the tiny entry hall, is an even tinier hall, leading directly to a bathroom. Two bedrooms bud off, one on each side, so that three doors open into the same space, or would except that all three open in instead of out. Even so there are occasional collisions in front of the bathroom.

As I attempted to settle Cameron in the front bedroom, reminding myself that we really needed to switch that so that Hal would have the larger bedroom and Cameron wouldn't be so near the street, I could hear Hal talking to Shane. About Lori, of course. What else? There was certainly nothing else on his mind these days.

Then I heard Harry's footsteps, followed by his voice saying, "Hal, why don't you go on up to the hospital? You can finish your history paper after you get home. Your Mom'll be up there about nine to take over."

Nine is when they run all visitors off in the intensive care area. Donna and I didn't count as visitors, because the nurses were so overloaded that having somebody to sit with Lori at least part of the time was—as they said—a big help. They ran us off at midnight most of the time, which is just as well, because otherwise neither Donna nor I would have gotten any sleep at all. As it was, Donna was up there at seven every morning that they wouldn't let her return right when she got off work at midnight, and I was up there as soon after four as possible, after working eight to four, a schedule that, because of muster, is actually seven-thirty to four. Hal, of course, was up there whenever he was allowed, which in practice was as much as possible of the interval between school's letting out at three-thirty and the staff's chasing him out at nine.

Enough of this. At least I had a chance to talk with Harry, which I hadn't done much of for the last two weeks, even if the talk couldn't be very private due to the presence of Shane. I sat down on the couch; I couldn't very well sit beside him because he was still—rather again—crouched over the computer. "I'm glad you let Hal go to the hospital."

"But he really does have to finish that homework," Harry said, and then winced as Shane discovered Hal's boom box. Fortunately Shane, unlike Hal, turned it down a little.

"Agreed," I said. "But he certainly won't do a decent job of it worrying about Lori."

"So letting him go to the hospital is going to stop him from worrying about Lori?" Harry said. "Hell, *I'm* worrying about Lori. Even the *dog* is worrying about Lori."

That was perfectly true. Donna, for some reason I couldn't begin to understand, had been growing—or seeming to grow—more and more distant over the last few months. Lori had spent a lot of time visiting her aunt, who lived six blocks from us.

Visiting her aunt, in effect, had meant living with us and going to her aunt's house to sleep. As always happens when a family changes composition, subtle shifts in loyalty had been taking place, and one of them, oddly enough, had resulted in the dog's apparent decision that Lori belonged to him. Every time she arrived he barked frantically until she went out to pet him and play with him, and on the days she didn't arrive somewhere in the neighborhood of four o'clock he would sit by the front gate and howl dismally.

He'd finally quit that, to the great relief of all the neighbors, but he still sat by the gate every day when the school bus arrived, and began whimpering when only Hal got off.

But I'd been married to Harry long enough to know that something besides Lori was eating him now. It could, of course, be his continuing unemployment. He was finishing his MBA preparatory to returning to Bell Helicopter as a supervisor instead of a test pilot, a job he could no longer manage since about two years ago, when a very new prototype tested out very poorly. To be precise, it sat down hard in a field, on its side, trapping Harry until a search-and-rescue unit could arrive and disentangle him.

It could be the MBA program, which definitely did not consist of snap courses.

I had a hunch it was neither of those. "You want to tell me what's wrong?" I asked.

"Oh, hell," he said, and doubled his right hand into a fist, which he slammed into his left palm.

I waited. Sooner or later he'd tell me, probably considerably sooner if I waited than if I tried to prod.

Finally he said, "That murder you're working on, that's Eric Huffman, right?"

"Right," I said. "You've been watching the news?"

"Uh-uh. I was when you called me about the kid, Shane Corbett. I recognized his name."

"Oh?"

"Yeah, Eric told me about him a couple of months ago."

"You knew Eric Huffman?"

"I knew Eric Huffman. He and I had been kind of working together to try to find the hacker."

"You'd been doing what?" I screamed. "Harry, how did you know about the hacker, before—?"

"It's been eating my computer," he said, totally incomprehensibly. "That . . . worm program. The virus. The one that messed up—"

"You mean computer hacker," I realized, remembering the pages of gibberish I'd seen in Eric's computer room, the gibberish that matched the gibberish spewed out by Harry's printer.

"What did you think I meant?"

"Never mind. Go on. The worm program, whatever that is, you and he were both trying to find whoever wrote it?"

"Yeah. It was spreading by modem."

"How long had you known Eric Huffman?" I asked.

"Oh, lord, years and years, I don't know," Harry said. "When I got into ham radio, I was with this net, you know, and Eric was with the same net. You ought to remember him, Deb, you met him at Lake Livingston a couple of years ago."

"I don't remember anybody I met at Lake Livingston." The main thing I remembered about the Lake Livingston trip, in fact, is that it took place in February, the weather was far too cold for me to feel comfortable camping out. I had absolutely nothing to say to any of the several hundred ham radio operators running about talking in code, and furthermore I was seven months pregnant. If you have never tried to use a sleeping bag and cook over a Coleman stove on the ground in February when you are seven months pregnant, let me tell you, you just don't know what you are missing.

Suddenly remembering that that trip wasn't my fondest memory, Harry went on rapidly. "We hadn't met face to face very much, but just, you know, talking. He dropped off the net a couple of years ago, and then when I got the computer I found him again; he'd moved over to computer a little before me."

I nodded, as Harry went on, "I'm really surprised anybody killed him. I can't see why anybody would want to. He was . . . he was kind of a nonentity. I can't see anybody feeling strongly enough about him to want to kill him. He was sort of... it's hard to know how to put it. He was sort of a gray man. You could be talking with him and forget he was there. Couldn't it have been a burglar or something? Somebody that broke in and didn't expect to find anybody home?''

"No, it wasn't a burglar," I said. "What do you know about him?"

"He was a retired lawyer. He'd had a heart attack a few years back and never did go back to full-time work. I don't know, I had the impression he was pretty well off, you know, not like Olead''— Olead is our multimillionaire son-in-law, the one who's a medical student—"but comfortable. Like it didn't matter whether he worked. He wasn't any kind of an outdoorsman—when we had that hamfest at Lake Livingston he used a motor home to drive down in. Are you sure you don't remember him?"

I still didn't remember him. But I did remember the motor home—vividly. As I tried to get myself and my midsection comfortable in a too-small sleeping bag on the hard ground, I had coveted that motor home.

"What did you think I meant when I said hacker?" Harry asked again.

I didn't want to tell him, not if Eric Huffman was a friend of his. But I might as well, because it was certainly going to be in the morning paper. "It was an ax murder," I disclosed reluctantly. "It was somebody who knew him. It was somebody who hated him." I stopped; Harry, his eyes wide with shock, was staring at me, shaking his head.

"Deb," he said, "*nobody* hated Eric Huffman. I'm telling you the truth. Nobody. Nobody would have had a reason. He's not...he wasn't the kind of guy anybody would care enough about to hate."

Somebody cared enough to hate him, I thought drearily, as I got up and went to the kitchen for a glass of water. "Harry, somebody did," I said, returning to the couch.

Harry shook his head. Then, in an obvious effort to change the subject, he asked, "How's Donna doing now?" He'd gone to the hospital with me that first night, but had hung back as Donna wept and I tried to comfort her.

I shrugged. "She's there." I thought about it a moment. "Sort of there. Sort of not there."

"I was afraid of that, the way she was carrying on," Harry said. "It just...Deb, she didn't seem to me to be steady enough to have any business being a police officer."

"She's usually okay," I said. "At least, as well as I know her." I didn't really know her well at all. Considering myself the potential mother-in-law of her daughter, considering her the potential mother-in-law of my son, I'd taken some trouble to get to know her, but the fact was that I was too busy to have much time to visit anybody, and she somehow didn't seem to like being visited. She never visited me; if she was going to pick up Lori at our house she just sat out in the car and honked. Most of the time Hal took Lori home; sometimes Harry or I did; but if either of us went in to try to visit, Donna always seemed a little too busy, or distracted in some way, to want to be visited.

"I don't think she's unsteady most of the time," I said. "She seems to do well enough on the job. But you do need to remember her husband was killed by a hit-and-run driver."

"I didn't know that." Harry, unlike me, was still drinking coffee, and he walked past me now and poured himself a cup. Returning not to the radio— excuse me, *computer*—table, but to the couch, he sat down beside me. "When did that happen?"

"About four years ago," I said.

"She was a police officer then? The same time her husband was?"

"Oh, yes. She'd been on the department a couple of years by then. What happened was, there'd been a pile-up on the freeway, during one of those ice storms we get in January, and her husband had been sent to try to get traffic around it, if that was possible, and the only way he had to get to it was to approach going the other way and park on the shoulder and walk across the median. He'd just gotten out of his car and was walking toward the pile-up, still in the other lane, when some car hit him and just kept on going."

"Killed on impact?" Harry asked.

"No, he was in the hospital, comatose, for about three weeks before he died."

"Shee-it," Harry said.

"Yeah. And now Lori's in the hospital comatose. So you can see why she—Donna, I mean—might be acting a little, well, strange."

Harry nodded. "I can't say I know how she feels. I don't, and I'm damn glad I don't." He glanced at the clock. "I guess if you're going to be up there by nine you'd better go and get ready. Though I still don't know what good it's doing."

"For Lori, no good at all," I agreed. "She's in intensive care; if she so much as wiggles there'll be a nurse there, with all the wiring and tubes they've got her hooked up to. But it makes Donna feel a little better—feel like somebody cares."

"But there ought to be somebody besides you and Donna to sit in the hospital," Harry said.

He was right, I thought as I put my shoulder holster back on and grabbed my crochet bag. There ought to be somebody besides Donna and me to sit in the hospital and wait all those interminable hours while Lori breathed and blips danced across screens. But there wasn't. No grandparents, no cousins, no uncles, no aunts—not even the aunt who lived near us, though that was understandable because she was in poor health—no friends. No friends, and that was what said the most, not about Lori, whose friends weren't old enough to take on that sort of a task, but about Donna. Maybe, once this was over and Lori was back to normal—I refused to think of any other possible outcome—Donna would make a little more time, take a little more trouble, to cultivate friends.

But who was I to criticize Donna, I thought guilty, as I absently patted the dog, locked the gate so the dog wouldn't get out, and scrambled into the car. Until a few years ago I hadn't had any friends either. Not real friends. Oh, acquaintances, plenty of acquaintances—the women whose husbands, like Harry, were active Elks. I'd sat at their bingo table whenever I went to play bingo, but I didn't do it very often because every time I went I nearly choked to death on the heavy smoke that always filled the huge room.

I sat with them when we had Elks banquets and that sort of thing, and of course the Elks Christmas party and the Elks New Year's dance, both of which involved the same room with a little less smoke and a lot more (and more elegant) drinks than the beer that was the most you could get with Bingo cards.

My friends were other police officers I'd worked with, and a few of their wives. But not many, because police wives tend to distrust policewomen. Policewomen spend too much time with police wives' husbands, in situations that could get involved, and anybody who thinks police officers—male or female—don't grow to love their partners—male or female—has never been in a situation where his (or her) life depends, day after day, on the same somebody else.

That's a different kind of love, though, and it almost never turns into romantic love. Policemen, and policewomen, know that. Police wives, and for that matter police husbands, often don't.

But really, really, did I know any of them—Elks wives, police wives—well enough to ask them to go and sit with an injured child in the hospital? Did any of them know me well enough to offer?

I knew better than that.

And of course the policemen and other policewomen wouldn't offer, because they, like I, had their plates full already.

To be honest with myself, I had to admit that even now I didn't have many friends except other police officers, and I didn't exactly pal around with any of them. There was Susan Braun, of course, but she couldn't go and sit with my child in the hospital—or with me, if it came to that—because she had her own patients to take care of.

May Rector, from the church Hal belongs to and I attend occasionally. She wouldn't be able to go sit in the hospital with one of my children, unless it was Cameron, because she'd be busy babysitting Cameron, a job she'd not volunteered for but rather had begged for. And I still had occasional doubts as to whether she was doing it out of friendship or because she still had hopes of converting me.

Sister Eagle Feather, whose real name was Matilda Greenwood?

She probably would, actually.

I'd met her in the course of an investigation a few months back, and we'd gotten to be pretty good friends. She was a qualified psychologist who insisted she was a real trance medium—that, I still had trouble believing—and who ran a spiritualist "church" so that she could reach depressed, grief-stricken people who wouldn't dream of going to a doctor for relief of depression. I wished, briefly, that I could talk Donna into going to see Sister Eagle Feather, but she wouldn't do that any more than she would go to a doctor.

Oh, well. I parked very carefully directly under a streetlight—I'm not crazy enough to go out into a dark parking lot by myself and get into a dark car at midnight, even if I am armed—and headed into the hospital.

Hal was sitting in the waiting room, which meant it was after nine o'clock and they'd chased him out of intensive care. Seeing me, he stood up and said, "I'm going home now."

"How's Lori?" I asked, not because I expected an informative answer but because Hal expected the question.

"Just about the same," he said. "Except she was a little wiggly. The nurse said that was good."

I nodded. "See how much of that homework you can finish up before bedtime," I said persuasively.

"Yeah," he replied, which meant exactly nothing.

Lori was noticeably restless for an hour or two, which was indeed a good sign; a comatose person getting restless might be about to wake up. But later she settled down, and I was dozing beside her bed when Donna came in at twelve-fifteen.

I woke up long enough to go home. Harry was asleep; Cameron was asleep; so—presumably—were Hal and Shane. The dog and cat, of course, weren't, and they escorted me to the front door, where the cat went in and the dog tried to.

It would be a lot easier just to allow the dog in the house, I thought, using a knee to block the entrance long enough for me to slip in. But Harry feels—probably correctly—that whatever the right place for a pit bull might be, it certainly isn't the living room—especially a living room occupied by sensitive electronic equipment easily knocked down by a dog who wags his entire hindquarters to make up for his lack of a tail.

FOUR

SATURDAY MORNING. I was not scheduled to work. I had to work anyway. But at least I didn't have to report in at seven-thirty, because I was not on duty. Eventually I'd get comp time for the time I worked, but no telling when that would be.

At least I had time for a decent breakfast—or what I considered a decent breakfast—instead of my usual weekday repast of Cheerios, bananas, and milk. I'd make apple-cinnamon-nut muffins, assuming, that is, that Hal had left me apples and pecans. The cinnamon I was sure of; I buy it by the very large box, because everybody in the family is addicted to cinnamon toast.

I had apples. I had pecans. What in the world was wrong with Hal's appetite? Worry, of course. I knew the answer to that, but what was puzzling me was that, although he doesn't gain weight on his usual twelve thousand calories a day, he was showing no signs at all of losing weight now, while he was eating a fraction of that.

Maybe he was less active?

Maybe he's so healthy that he stays a normal weight no matter what he eats?

If so, what an enviable problem.

Putting Weight Watchers margarine on four enormous muffins sprinkled with cinnamon and sugar and topped with pecans is probably an exercise in futility, but it was delicious all the same. The baby got muffins too, but with the pecans removed, he doesn't yet have enough teeth to be trusted with nuts.

After breakfast Shane asked where the closest bus stop was; he thought he'd go job hunting today.

"On Saturday?" Harry asked.

"Well, restaurants, they hire on Saturday too," Shane said. "Uh...you got a quarter you could give me, like, for bus fare?"

"You're not going to get far for a quarter," Harry pointed out.

"I thought maybe I could ask somebody else for the rest of it," Shane said meekly.

Harry checked his pockets and handed over two dollars. "But it's more than a mile to the closest bus stop," he warned.

Shane shrugged. "I'll hoof it. I've done it before."

"I'm going to the hospital," Hal said. "I can drop you off downtown. Then you'll just have to take the bus back. If, uh, if I can have the truck?"

"Take the truck," Harry said resignedly. "Be back by noon, to hit that homework again."

"I will," Hal assured him.

"How about if I go with you to the hospital?" Shane was saying as he went out the door. "Then I can see your girl, and then I can go and see if maybe the hospital wants some help in their kitchen—"

Like they were going to be hiring on Saturday, I thought but did not say.

"Yeah," I heard Hal answer. "You can meet Lori's mom, she's always up there right now, and she'll be real glad to meet you, and—"

Right, I thought. Absolutely right. Just what Donna needed—to meet Shane. Dandy.

Hal and Shane were both well out the door before I had time to think of the breakfast dishes.

Unfortunately, it doesn't take long to put dishes in the dishwasher, and after that I could think of no more reasons for stalling. That meant that I had to ascertain the whereabouts of Clara Huffman (that's police jargon for find out where she was) and go and talk to her.

A telephone call to the hospital revealed that Clara Huffman was back at home. I couldn't imagine why she'd have wanted to go there; the murder scene couldn't possibly have been cleaned yet, because we weren't ready to release it. Maybe the hospital was wrong about where she'd gone. After all, their records would show that she was released, but not necessarily where she had gone after her release.

But a telephone call to the house revealed that Clara Huffman really had gone there, and was willing to talk with me, although she couldn't see how it would do any good.

Rats. That got rid of my last excuse for staying home.

I telephoned Irene, to let her know that Clara was home and we could go finish searching the house. I could hear her smug smile even over the telephone. "I finished last night," she said.

"You what?"

"I finished that last night. I didn't see any reason why it should wait any longer. And we still had the consent to search. I just got the victim's key out of property and Sarah and I went over there and finished up."

"Find anything useful?"

"Depends on what you consider useful. We did not find anything even remotely resembling a possible murder weapon."

Which meant the perpetrator had taken it with him or her. That thought didn't exactly make my day.

But at least I didn't have to search the house besides talking with the widow.

I made one more telephone call before leaving, this time to Methodist Hospital to ask Donna how Lori was doing—about the same, she said—and to tell her I really couldn't come to the hospital today.

"You've got your family to take care of," she agreed. "Don't worry. I'll manage."

That, of course, had the paradoxical effect of making me feel worse instead of better. Does everybody have to choose all the time between two or three things, all of which *must* be done, I wondered as I assured the dog I really had to go, or am I the only one?

Actually, I knew the answer to that. Every woman who works outside her home—and I knew perfectly well that the phrase "working mother" is a bad joke; every mother is a working mother—is bound to feel torn in two periodically. Normally I wasn't any—well, not much—worse off than anybody else; it was just that my conflicts were a little more obvious.

And right now I *had* to take care of my baby, before he forgot what I looked like; and I *had* to try to console Hal and Donna and help to sit with Lori, because the hospital had asked Donna to try to have somebody with her all the time; and I *had* to solve this murder, because let's face it, an ax murderer is often known to be a repeater.

Of course there were other people to do all of those things. But I was—at least in my own mind— the one who was *supposed* to be doing them.

All right, I had decided which of the three was not more important, perhaps, but certainly more urgent. Having made the decision, the least I could do was try to be cheerful about it. Mrs. Huffman, I told myself as I parked in front of her house, had enough trouble without me walking around looking like a thundercloud.

Clara Huffman was calmer than she had been seventeen hours ago, but somehow she seemed older, frailer. Her blue-gray hair was neatly brushed, now, but all traces of the bouffant hairdo of yesterday had vanished. She was wearing a flannelette housecoat over a flannelette nightgown, and she hadn't put on any makeup. Without it, the blueness of her face was far more evident; she must have been older than I would have guessed yesterday, perhaps considerably older.

"It was that awful boy, of course," she told me without the preamble of a greeting. She turned back from the door and seated herself fairly gracefully on that lovely decorator couch.

"Boy?" I queried, sitting down on a matching chair.

"That...*Shane,*" she spat, making the word sound like profanity. And yet, despite the surface anger, I felt some lack of emotion under her voice, as if she were only partially present. "I told Eric we had no business taking in a street person like that. They're all criminals. If they weren't, what would they be doing living on the street?"

I could think of several thousand answers to that, ranging from mental illness to prolonged unemployment, but it wouldn't do any good to give them. Abruptly I did not like Clara Huffman as much as I had earlier. "What makes you think it was Shane?" I asked.

"Who else would it have been?"

"That's what we need to find out," I replied. "Suppose it was Shane, why would he have wanted to do it? Eric—Mr. Huffman—had taken him in, been kind to him.''

''Ungrateful, that's what he was. Young people are all so ungrateful.''

''Perhaps. But ingratitude is rarely a motive for murder.'' It is sometimes, of course, she's right about that. For a moment I let myself think of Dr. Ezra Loundes, psychiatrist, philanthropist, murdered along with his wife by two drifters they'd taken in. But those were drug-related kills, and I'd have bet anything anybody cared to name that Shane wasn't into drugs. ''There must have been some other reason.''

She looked around, vaguely. ''Maybe Shane was trying to steal all that computer stuff, and Eric walked in and found him.''

''Then why did he demolish the computer equipment? Once Mr. Huffman was dead, he could have just taken it with him.''

''Maybe...maybe he was panicky. People get panicky, you know.''

''Maybe,'' I said. ''But I need to explore some other possibilities.''

''What for? Why don't you just go and arrest that boy?''

I took a deep breath and started to explain probable cause to her.

''What about the ax?'' she asked when I got through.

''What ax is that? We haven't found one.''

"We had one. Eric used it for chopping firewood, years ago, before he got so sick. Of course, we buy firewood now, already cut. It's not here anymore, the ax, I mean. I looked. If . . . if that was what he used, then he must have taken it with him."

"Whoever it was," I agreed. "That's certainly worth thinking about. Can you show me where it was kept?"

She looked around again, still vaguely. "I don't remember. Last time I saw it . . ." She paused for a moment. "Last time I saw it, it was in Eric's study. That's odd. I wonder what it could have been doing there?"

"Was that before or after Eric was killed?"

"You know, I don't remember. That's odd, too. Why wouldn't I remember that?"

There were several possibilities. One was that the ax was still in the study when she found the body, and was removed later. If that were true, then the killer—whoever the killer was—was still here when Clara arrived, and slipped out later, before the first police got here.

Another was that Clara had killed Eric herself and then blanked it out, all except a vague memory of seeing the ax in Eric's study. But I didn't believe that. I wasn't prepared to believe that, not without a lot of investigation.

"Somebody took the towels, too," she added fretfully. "And got all kinds of black dirt in the bathroom."

"Did they? Maybe I'd better have a look." I knew what I'd find. No matter who did it, that person hadn't left this house without cleaning up. Irene knew that as well as I did, and she'd have searched the bathroom very thoroughly for blood, for fingerprints, for any place where the weave of the killer's clothing might have been traced on the bathroom floor in drying blood while the killer bathed.

Indeed, the towels were gone. So was the shower curtain. Clara Huffman was lucky to have a sink left. But there was no evidence tape on this room, so Irene must have been through with it. I located a linen closet and got out clean towels, found a rag, and swished the worst of the fingerprint powder off the sink and the tiling. When I returned to the living room, Clara blinked. For a moment I wondered if she'd forgotten I was here. But then she asked, "What did you say, dear?"

"Never mind," I said. "It wasn't important. Do you mind if I go and look in Eric's study again, before we go on with this conversation?"

"Go ahead. I believe I need some more coffee." Halfway into the kitchen, she paused to ask, "Would you like some?"

"No, thank you," I said. "I'm out of the habit of coffee." She was puzzling me more and more. Yesterday she'd been hysterical at the thought of remaining in this house; today she didn't seem to care. I saw no sign of alcohol, but she had that strange detachedness that so often accompanies extreme intoxication. Of course, the doctor probably had her on some kind of sedative. I'd check on that.

The murder room—Eric's study, Clara Huffman called it—looked just the same as I remembered it looking. Not a pleasant sight. I didn't break or cut the yellow tape across the doorway, the tape that said KEEP OUT! CRIME SCENE! I didn't have to. I reached under the tape to open the door inward, then stood at the tape to look into the room. What I saw confirmed what I thought I remembered. The way the blood had rained around that room, it was clear that the killer had not stayed in one spot, so that his or her body would be outlined in blood. No, the killer had moved around, walking or running. It was impossible for anyone to have moved around in that havoc without being not just spattered but virtually drenched in blood.

Suppose, for the sake of argument, that Clara Huffman had done it. She couldn't have done it after her hair appointment, because what was left of the nice hairdo, tousled as it had become, had still been visible when she left with the doctor. If she had done it before she left for the appointment, she would have had to bathe and wash her hair. What had she looked like when she arrived at the appointment? People with standing hair appointments don't usually wash their hair at home at all. Her hairdresser would be able to say whether or not she'd arrived with last week's hairdo still partially in place.

That, I would have to check on, just for the sake of ruling her out definitely. But I was willing to bet I knew what the hairdresser would say.

I followed Clara Huffman into the kitchen just in time to see her swallowing something from a prescription bottle. "May I see that?" I asked.

She handed the bottle to me and looked around vaguely—always vaguely. Yesterday there'd been nothing vague about her; today I'd almost have been ready to call her senile, especially when she asked, "What was I going to do?"

"You came in here to make coffee," I said, and looked at the bottle. XANAX. TAKE ONE EVERY FOUR HOURS. And that explained the vagueness. My doctor once prescribed Xanax for me, as a muscle relaxant, after I'd sprained my back. By the time I had taken two of them, I was doing well to remember my own name. My short-term memory was totally gone—I couldn't find my car keys, my billfold, or my pistol; I couldn't remember what I had put in the oven; I once overflowed the bathtub because I turned the water on and then couldn't remember why I was undressing. My long-term memory wasn't much better. After Harry called the doctor (Harry had to—I couldn't find the telephone), I no longer took Xanax. It took me about four days to get back to normal.

A very loud crack jerked my attention back to the moment, and I turned to see Clara Huffman staring stupidly at a broken glass coffee carafe in her hand. She'd taken it off its heat source and immediately run cold water in it.

"You sit down; I'll make you the coffee," I said, mentally swearing at Dr. Smiley for being so irresponsible as to send her home alone in this condition. But then he probably hadn't expected her to be alone. Most people wouldn't be. Was she another social isolate, like Donna—like me?

"How did you get home from the hospital?" I asked, my back to her as I searched counters and shelves for something to make coffee in and with.

"I took a taxi," she said. "It cost thirty dollars. I gave the driver fifty. Was that too much?"

"Probably," I said absently. I haven't checked taxi fares lately, but it did seem to me that even thirty dollars, let alone fifty, was quite a lot for a ride that couldn't have been over ten miles at most.

I couldn't find another carafe, but there was an electric percolator in a shelf under the counter. Her coffee grind seemed to be for electric drip pots, but I felt sure it wouldn't demolish the universe to use the stuff in a percolator.

Moments later, with the plopping of the percolator in the background, I sat down with her at the table. "Do you have a friend I could call to come stay with you?" I asked.

"Oh, I'm all right," she said. "I'll be driving to the funeral home in an hour or so anyway."

"Mrs. Huffman, didn't the doctor tell you not to drive while you're taking that medicine?"

"Oh, yes, but I'll be all right."

It would be tantamount to murder for me to leave her alone in this house, unless I took with me every car key in the place, which didn't seem very practical. "Where is your address book, Mrs. Huffman?"

"You don't need to worry about me," she said airily.

"Mrs. Huffman, where is your address book?"

"In the telephone stand."

She moved toward the coffeepot, and I headed her off. "It's not ready yet. I'll pour you some when it is."

I picked a name at random out of the address book. Well, not totally at random. Mardee Hamilton, only a couple of miles away, seemed to be the nearest, if not closest, of her friends.

Mardee Hamilton sounded about my age, maybe a little older, and she was somewhat alarmed to learn that Clara—on a strong tranquilizer—was by herself. She promised to arrive within half an hour, and to stay as long as was necessary. There wasn't any family, she told me, but she'd see to it Clara wasn't left alone. She'd have come over sooner, but when she telephoned she didn't get any answer, and assumed Clara was in the hospital. "I used to be

Eric's secretary, when he had an office that wasn't at home," she told me, "and I know them both quite well. I was...most distressed to hear what happened."

"Who notified you?" I asked.

"Nobody. I learned it from the ten o'clock news. That...shocked me, because I would have expected to be called, but then I realized of course Clara was hysterical."

"Does Clara frequently get hysterical?"

"Oh, yes," Mardee Hamilton said. "And it isn't put on. She's always been—I hope this makes sense—emotionally frail. That's one of the reasons they didn't have children. Well...Ms....Ralston, you said?"

"That's right."

"I was just lounging around the house this morning, so I'd better go and get dressed. I'll be there as quickly as possible. Please don't leave before I get there."

"I'll certainly wait," I promised her, and hung up.

While I had the address book, I took a moment to copy the name and telephone number of the hairdresser. I could almost certainly settle at least one question with a five-minute phone call a little later in the day.

Returning to the kitchen, I poured Clara Huffman a cup of coffee, saw to it there was enough milk in it that she couldn't scald herself if she spilled it, and resumed asking questions.

I didn't get much in the way of answers, not that I expected much in view of her present condition. Everything I did get bore out what we already had.

Eric had been an attorney, semi-retired. He'd never done any criminal work. He'd never been involved in any real litigation, just saw to it contracts were properly written and that kind of thing. He'd never had to worry about money, because both Eric and Clara were only children with wealthy parents. Clara had never held a job outside the home, but while Eric was in practice she'd done his bookkeeping for him. Yes, she was a trained bookkeeper, and she rather enjoyed it. No, she hadn't done it lately; once he got the computer he began to do it himself on the computer. Yes, she knew about the computer hacker and the virus; Eric had been really mad about it, but he'd gotten it cleared up days ago. Yes, he had had a lot of hobbies. No, she didn't ever go with him to hamfests or anything like that; she'd gone a couple of times years ago and they bored her.

And again and again, the same thing I'd heard from her before, the same thing I'd heard from Harry. Nobody would have hated Eric enough to murder him. The murder had to be for some other reason.

If this continued I was going to begin to believe it myself. But the fact remained that the man *had* been murdered, and I'd never heard of an ax murder that wasn't a personal kill.

Names of friends. No enemies. No reason. No reason. No *reason*.

Mardee Hamilton arrived, another slender well-dressed woman with blue-gray hair, and took over quite efficiently, steering Clara in the direction of the bed, where she obviously needed to be. I decided to stick around for a while. This woman might be worth talking to.

Mardee returned to the kitchen. "She's asleep," she told me, "but I don't know how long she'll stay that way. A few hours, anyway. I appreciate your staying."

"I had more than one reason," I said. "Would you mind if I ask you some questions?"

"Not at all." She reached for a coffee cup and a spoon, with none of the fumbling and opening wrong doors and drawers that I had done. Clearly, I thought, she knew this house.

"How long were you Mr. Huffman's secretary?" I asked.

"Twenty years," she said precisely, sitting down and holding the cup in both hands. No wedding ring, I noticed; no rings at all except a large square-cut topaz on her right hand. "Actually a little over."

"Was Mrs. Huffman ever..." I paused, looking for a delicate way to ask. "Jealous of you, the way some women are of their husband's secretaries?"

She looked startled, and then laughed. "What's your name again? Ralston? Detective Ralston?"

"Yes. Most people call me Deb."

"Then you should call me Mardee. No, Deb, Clara was not jealous of me. She had no reason to be. I'm the very best kind of a secretary for the husband of a very...insecure woman."

I suppose I looked puzzled, because Mardee laughed again. "I'm not the least bit interested in men, you see. If I were, then she—Clara—would be threatened. Or if I were a male secretary she could feel threatened, because who knows, I might be gay and then she might be threatened. But as it is, well...no need to worry. See?"

That took me a minute to digest, and then I suppose I blushed, because she said, "Let me guess. You must be a Baptist, right? One of those fundamentalist Texas Baptists?"

"No, Mormon," I replied, "and not particularly fundamentalist." Then I wondered again why I kept saying I was a Mormon when in fact I wasn't. Maybe May Rector and the others like her were doing a better job of converting me than I thought they were.

"Oh, my!" Mardee said, in a mockingly malicious tone. "Then you're undoubtedly convinced I'm going absolutely straight to hell-fire."

"Actually I'm not," I replied. "Look, you're protesting against my judging you when I'm not, but you're judging me—without any hearing, I might add. Don't tell me what I think. I know what I think. You don't." Then, with perhaps a little malice myself, I said, "Agreed that Clara didn't have any reason to feel threatened. Did Eric?"

Mardee lifted one eyebrow. *"Her?* You're asking me if I was ever interested in *Clara?"* She paused for a minute. "No. Look...try to understand this. Some people are strong. They're to be congratulated. Some people could be strong and decided not to be. They're to be scorned. Then there are the ones like Clara. She couldn't be strong if she had to be. If she had to be strong or be...eaten by a tiger, let's say...she'd sit there and let the tiger eat her. She'd cry when she saw the tiger coming, but that's all. I pity her. I'm sorry for her. And no, I'm not going to let her drive as long as she's taking Xanax—always assuming she could find her car keys, that is, which I wouldn't bet for a minute. As I said, I pity her. But interested in her? No way."

That was believable to me. "Who do you think might have hated Eric enough to kill him?"

Her answer was the same as everybody else's, and it came just as fast. "Nobody," she said. "Nobody at all. He...you never saw him alive, so it's hard for me to explain him to you. He was...there, but he wasn't there. Not quite. You know all those hobbies of his, the CB radios and the ham radios and the computer nets and so forth? You know why he had to do all that stuff? Because he couldn't get anybody to talk with him more than five minutes face to face, that's why. He had less presence than anybody else I ever saw in my life."

"Then why did you work for him for twenty years?"

"It paid well," she said. "Paid very, very well; the work wasn't hard; and it left me plenty of time to myself to do things that were more challenging, and probably some of it would have paid better. But then I wouldn't have had nearly so much *me* time. And you may consider this a narcissistic statement, Deb Ralston, but I need a lot of me time."

I could certainly understand that; I needed a lot of me time, too. In hopes of getting through this case quickly, in order to have a little of that me time this weekend, I went through the same questions again, and got the same depressing answers. Nobody hated Eric Huffman. Nobody even disliked him. Nobody could remember he was there long enough to dislike him.

A few more questions, this time looking at cui bono, who benefits from the death. "They have no family," Mardee said. "He wrote their wills himself and I typed and witnessed them. Each of them left everything to the other, and the residuary legatee was the Amon Carter Museum."

Even my imagination, powerful though it undoubtedly is, could not conjure up a vision of a trustee of the Amon Carter Museum committing an ax murder to lay hands on an estate a few years early, especially when the primary legatee was still alive. And obviously Clara Huffman had had full use of her husband's money as well as her own as long as he had been alive. Even a divorce wouldn't have hurt her much, considering Texas is a community property state.

Motives for murder. Profit. Nobody profited to any measurable degree. Hatred. From all I could tell, nobody hated Eric Huffman. Jealousy. By whom? Of whom?

"Was Eric Huffman a philanderer?" I asked.

Mardee sipped her coffee. "Not that I know of. And if he'd been while I was working for him, I'd have known."

She probably would have known. Secretaries do.

While there was no obvious reason for anybody to murder Eric Huffman, the fact remained that somebody *had* murdered him, in a way that almost certainly was personal, a way that suggested extremely strong feeling.

"Is it okay if I clean up the study while she's asleep?" Mardee asked. "If she gets a good look at it when she gets out from under the Xanax, there'll be hell to pay. She'll go catatonic or something."

"Then keep the door closed," I said. "It can't be cleaned until we take the evidence tape off, and we're a long way from ready to do that yet."

I ought to have gone in to the police station and read the lab reports, but I decided to wait till later. They weren't going to tell me anything I didn't already know. Nobody could have begun looking at fingerprint evidence yet, even supposing there was any, because even if Eric Huffman had been printed for elimination (and he probably had been, in the morgue), Clara Huffman certainly hadn't been, and neither had Shane Corbett. Nobody was going to start searching prints until known ones were eliminated.

We didn't have the murder weapon. The lab might well know by now what had been used, which might help later in getting a conviction, but it certainly wasn't going to be anything likely to lead me to *who* right now.

Beyond that, what could the lab tell me? That Eric Huffman had been murdered extremely messily. That there was a lot of blood around, and a lot of bone and skull and brain tissue. That a computer setup also had been hacked to pieces, and there was a lot of plastic and glass and electronic components mixed in with the blood. Nothing, as I said, that I didn't already know.

Captain Millner would say I should have gone and read the lab reports anyway.

But I didn't. I went to the grocery store and bought some frozen pizzas and some frozen pot pies and some canned soup and some milk and frozen vegetables and frozen fruit and bread and toilet paper, and then I went home and picked up the baby.

Holding him, I called Clara Huffman's hairdresser, asked the questions I'd planned to ask, and got the answers I'd expected.

Clara was on time for her appointment. She didn't seem agitated or upset in any way. The remains of her last week's hairdo, including a lot of teasing, were visibly in place.

If Clara Huffman killed her husband, she must have worn a space suit to do it in.

Not that I'd really suspected her to start with.

That done, I settled down with the baby in my lap and a glass of milk and the leftover muffins (so far had Hal sunk—there were actually muffins left over) to read and listen to the stereo.

After a while, Harry disengaged himself from the computer and asked, "Well? Learn anything yet?"

"Uh-uh," I said, my mouth full of muffins.

"My," Cameron announced, reaching past me.

"Your what?" I asked.

"My bobble." He grabbed my glass of milk but slightly misjudged how far to tip it, it being at least three times the size of the glasses he is allowed to use, to say nothing of being heavy glass rather than light plastic. He upended it, drenching both him and me. I jumped up, the glass broke, both cats came running to drink the spilled milk and at once began fighting over it, and Cameron, still in my arms, began to howl.

At least Harry cleaned up the glass and put the cats outside while I washed Cameron and me.

"Now, let's get this straight," I said half an hour later, in the kitchen. *"This* is your bobb—I mean, bottle." I set a bottle on the counter. "This is your glass." A small yellow plastic juice glass. "This is *my* glass."

"My gass," Cameron said obediently, reaching for the quart-size iced-tea glass.

"No, no," I said. "Look. Cameron's glass. Mommy's glass."

"Cameron gass." He reached for the iced-tea glass again.

It took a while before I finally gave up and resigned myself to keeping all large glasses out of reach for the next two or three years. Then I put Cameron on the floor, turned on the oven, and started getting pot pies out. Then I paused. "Where's Hal?" I asked.

"We compromised," Harry said. "I let him go back to the hospital, providing he did his homework there."

"You think he really will?"

"He's sure not doing it here. He might do it there."

"I hope," I said dubiously. "Where's Shane?"

"He called and said he had a date and he'd be in later."

I looked rather ruefully at the twelve pot pies I had on the counter. "How many pot pies do you want?"

"What kind? Chicken or beef?"

"Chicken. The small ones."

"Oh, three, I guess," Harry said. "Is that okay?"

"Yeah."

Three for Harry, one for me, one for the baby—for Cameron, whom I was really going to have to stop calling "the baby." Oh, well, the others would keep. But I was glad I had asked before I started opening cartons.

After a while I remembered what else I'd meant to do, and I went and asked Harry what Eric had told him about Shane.

Harry yawned. "Eric told me he was a good ol' boy but wasn't worth a plugged penny."

"A what?"

"That's what I asked. And Eric told me a plugged penny is worth less than a plugged nickel. That's why I said it was okay to bring him home. Eric was . . . easy to ignore. But he was a good judge of character, I always thought. If there'd been anything wrong with Shane, except for pure bone laziness, Eric would have spotted it."

"So if I told you Eric's wife says Shane is the killer—"

"I'd say she was full of prunes. That's jealousy talking."

"That's what?"

"Eric said that was two-thirds of the reason he'd retired. Said it had gotten where Clara—that's his wife's name, Clara—"

"I know," I said impatiently.

"That's right, you would. Well, he said Clara had gotten where she was jealous of anybody or anything that took up any of his time at all."

That was interesting…except that on the basis of physical evidence, I'd already ruled Clara out.

HAL DRAGGED IN at nine-thirty, and it was frightening to see how utterly exhausted, drained, he looked. "I finished everything but the English paper," he said. "I'll do that tomorrow."

I doubt his ability to write a decent English paper in one day at the best of times, and this was far from the best of times. But I decided not to say so.

"How is she doing, son?" Harry asked.

Hal shook his head. "She wasn't wiggly today. She was just . . . just lying there. Like she was dead. Like she was already dead."

"Are you going to church in the morning, or straight back to the hospital?" I asked.

"Church first. I guess this would be a pretty crummy time to stop going to church. The Young Women's president came by today."

Lori had been going to church with Hal. Her mother wouldn't let her join, but had no problem with her going. "What did she say?" I asked. "The Young Women's president, I mean?"

Hal shook his head. "Nothing much. She offered to sit with Lori, but Lori's mom wouldn't let her. What else is there to say?"

He got a glass of milk and went to his room. He did not turn on the boom box. After a while the light went out, but I wouldn't want to gamble that he was sleeping.

THE DOG, PAT, started barking about two A.M., and then the doorbell rang. I got up and stumbled to the door, but Hal was ahead of me.

"Sorry," Shane said, "I guess I'm later than I meant to be."

He turned on the bedroom light and Cameron, disturbed, began to howl. I changed his diaper and cravenly gave him the nighttime bottle the pediatrician says he's not supposed to have anymore. Then I sneaked off to bed.

Hal and Shane were still talking when I dozed off again.

FIVE

IN MY EXPERIENCE, very few murders happen between two A.M. and five A.M. I don't really know why; my theory is that by two A.M. the late drunks either have reached the falling-down stage, in which they couldn't kill if they wanted to, or have gone somewhere to sleep it off, and by five A.M. the early drunks are waking up headachy, grouchy, and mean.

That does not, however, mean that earlier murders can't be *discovered* between two and five A.M.

When the phone rang at three-thirty A.M. I was pretty sure it was for me. I considered not answering it, but last time I tried that Captain Millner sent somebody to knock on my door. But considering that I hadn't gone to bed until after eleven, and had already been awakened about two by Shane, I wasn't in top form as I picked up the receiver. "H'lo?" I said.

"De-e-b, come to Papa." Not even the dispatcher. Millner himself.

"Oh, come on, have a heart," I protested. "I've already got all the murders I can handle."

"Now you've got another one."

"Why me? Isn't there anybody else?"

"You'll see when you get here. Helen's Club, on Camp Bowie. Upsy-daisy."

I could strangle him when he gets in that sort of a mood; he's bad enough when he's normal. But obviously I was getting up, whether I wanted to or not.

Unusually, I hadn't even laid out clothes the night before. That meant I had to go into the bathroom, close the door to avoid disturbing Harry, turn on the bathroom light, and decide what to wear. (Harry's and my clothes closets are located in two corners of the bathroom). Slacks. A sweatshirt. No, I definitely was *not* going to put on a decent pants suit at this hour of the alleged morning. My shoulder holster. A jacket—a new one I had bought recently. I love it. It's gray poplin and has eight pockets, all of them closing with Velcro so that nothing can get shaken out of the pockets. So I put my billfold, complete with driver's license and police ID, in one pocket and my notebook and tape measure in another pocket, and off I went, without having to worry about a purse at all. As useful as this jacket has become, for once I'll be halfway sorry when winter ends and I have to go back to carrying a purse.

When I came out the front door, Pat stood up, stretched his hindquarters, stretched his forequarters, and politely intimated that he'd like to go with me. "You'll have to sit in the car when I get there," I told him.

He whined.

"What the heck," I said. I stepped back into the house and grabbed his leash—not that any leash was going to hold Pat unless he agreed to be held; the average pit bull can tow a jeep for a short distance. Returning to the yard, I opened the back door of the old Escort I had bought to replace the old Lynx when it died. Pat hopped in, wagging his hindquarters until he got all the way into the car, at which point he had no more room to wag anything.

One thing about it, I reflected, escorted by a pit bull I ought to be safe. If someone wanted to hassle me I wouldn't even have to show my badge or pistol. A pit bull lifting one corner of his mouth to show his teeth, meanwhile saying, "Rrr-rrr-rrr," tends to be very, very intimidating even to the most determined of hasslers. Pat has never bitten anybody. But then, he has never needed to.

Pat whined when I got out of the car and shut the door, but I wasn't about to let him join me at a crime scene.

Helen's Club, a fairly trendy French restaurant-bar combination, would have closed about one A.M. on Saturday night—actually, of course, Sunday morning. Sometime between then and three A.M.—but probably closer to three than one, because Helen Thorne herself was apparently the only one left in the building—someone had entered through an unlocked back door. The twelve-to-eight beat cop, Andy Ryan, standing unhappily by the back door, told me that, when I stopped to talk with him. "I went to rattle her door and it came open," he said. "And man! I never seen anything like that before."

"Anything like what? Robbery and murder?" I asked. The combination is not what you'd call everyday, in Fort Worth or anywhere else, but it's by no means unheard of.

"Robbery? I don't think so. But it's sure as hell the damnedest murder I ever saw, and I've been on this department five years. Watch out for footprints," he added, as I turned toward the door.

I glanced down. Sneaker prints—on concrete, not pressed into dirt. Sneaker prints printed in blood. Somebody had walked through a lot of blood before coming out that door. More blood than usually results from a shooting, though I've seen stabbings in which the victim bled dry. All of a sudden I had a funny feeling that I knew what I was going to find and why Millner had decided to call me out.

Have you ever been in the back of a fancy restaurant? It doesn't look like the front. You've got the kitchens, of course, and generally they're nice and clean and shiny, at least after they've been cleaned for the night. But behind the public facade, behind the clean, shiny kitchens, you've got the receiving area, and that's usually concrete floors and wood or metal shelves smelling at least a little bit of onions that should have been cooked two weeks ago or thrown away a week ago, and you've got the office, and if you know what the office of a shade-tree mechanic looks like, with papers stacked around like they've been collecting since Noah's Ark grounded and never ever filed, well, a lot of the time that's what the far back of the fancy restaurant looks like, except with the sticky dust of cooking oil residue instead of the black oil of car repairs.

Helen Thorne—if this was Helen Thorne, and Ryan said there was nobody else in the restaurant—was indisputably dead.

So was her computer.

Except that the surroundings were so different and the victim was female, not male, this was a clone of the murder of Eric Huffman. And apparently my nice theory that Eric Huffman was killed for personal reasons had just gone up in smoke, because what personal reasons could exist for the murder of a retired lawyer on the northwest side of town and the murder of a restaurateur on Camp Bowie Boulevard?

"Ah, shit," I said.

"You took the words right out of my mouth," Captain Millner told me.

"Knock it off," I said. "This isn't funny."

"Deborah, my dear, of all the things it could possibly be considered, 'funny' is definitely not on the list."

"My name isn't Deborah and you know it. Has the ME been here yet?"

"Negative. I think Habib is coming. And Olsen."

Habib—Dr. Habib—is the pathologist I work with most often, and Richard Olsen is one of his two best investigators; Gil Sanchez is the other.

"Who's coming from ident?"

"Bob Castle."

"So in the meantime we wait."

"In the meantime we wait," Millner agreed.

That was obvious; we certainly couldn't go wandering through the office looking at—or for—things until after the crime scene work had been concluded, and at this time of night, on an otherwise deserted street, what else was there to do besides wait? There wasn't anybody we could go ask questions of.

"I'm going to hunt tire tracks," I said.

Millner nodded. "Keep your eyes open." He wasn't referring to my looking for tire tracks, but to my watching out for my own safety. That was something I was, unfortunately, notoriously bad about doing.

"I brought my secret weapon," I said smugly.

Millner turned, only mildly interested. "What's that?"

"Come on and I'll show you."

He followed me to the car. I opened the front door, grabbed the leash and my big flashlight, opened the back door, put my knee (which was also balancing the flashlight) between the door and the ground until I got the leash onto Pat's collar, and then retrieved the flashlight and backed away. Pat hopped out of the car, looked up at Captain Millner, curled one corner of his lip, and said, "Rrr-rrr-rr."

"Friend," I said hastily. "Let him smell your hand."

"You're sure he won't bite it off?" Millner asked, but dubiously extended his hand.

Pat quit saying, "Rrr-rrr-rr," sniffed the hand, looked at me, and then wagged his hindquarters.

"Anybody ever told you those kinds of dogs are dangerous?" Millner asked me.

"Only if they're abused, or trained to be," I replied. "German shepherds and Dobermans kill and injure a lot more people every year than pit bulls do." I didn't mention that Pat is only half pit bull. His other half is Doberman. I did say that in my opinion, it would make more sense to ban people who train pit bulls to be vicious than to ban pit bulls.

"Be that as it may," Captain Millner replied, "keep him away from me."

Pat and I, complete with flashlight, walked from one end of the block to the other. There were a lot of places where cars had parked. There was no reason to assume any of the cars was more likely to be the killer's car than any other.

What else to do? I led Pat back to where the bloody footprints tapered off, obviously because the blood had been walked off. "Find," I told Pat. I had been working at training Pat to be useful, in what little free time I had managed to produce over the last year.

He sniffed the footprints, wagged his tail, and whined. That sent an extremely mixed message to me, especially when he sniffed along the ground straight to the police car, stopped, and stood beside it wagging his hindquarters.

"Pat, you dope, I know where the police car is!" I said. "What about the footprints?"

I took him back to the beginning of the footprints, carefully holding his leash to the side to be sure he didn't tread directly on the prints. "Find," I told him again.

"Find" had been a game all summer and into the fall. He'd "found" Harry and me, Hal and Lori, and each time the "find" had been followed by rewards. Pat does not demand doggie biscuits as a reward; being petted or allowed to kiss people (which he does very sloppily) was sufficient.

He sniffed the footprints diligently. He followed the bloody line. Where the blood was no longer visible, at least to people, he went right on sniffing and occasionally whining. And once again he wound up at the police car. This time he tried to get in it.

Even if I had believed, which I did not, that Andy Ryan had reason to murder Helen Thorne and Eric Huffman, one glance was sufficient to tell me that Ryan had on regulation uniform shoes, not sneakers, and furthermore his foot was much too big to fit into the sneakers that made the trail of prints. Nor, as in the case of Eric Huffman, would it have been possible for anyone to commit this murder without being literally covered in blood.

Ergo, either Pat was confused, which is not at all impossible—he is not the world's most intelligent dog—or else the killer's car had been parked in exactly the same place that the police car was now parked. And that theory made perfectly good sense. Why not? In the alley behind the restaurant, it was certainly not visible from the street, and if for any reason the killer expected the back door to be open, then parking right at it was certainly sensible.

I started to ask Ryan to move the police car, but on second thought I decided not to. That could wait; we had the ME's car, the ME's investigator's car, and the crime scene car still to arrive, and if Ryan moved almost certainly somebody else would park there.

The first of those cars was nosing into the alley now; as I could see nothing but headlights, of course I couldn't tell who it was, until it moved up along the other side of the alley and parked directly behind the door, not leaving room for another car to get between it and the parked car.

Andrew Habib got out. "What have you—"

He was going to say "What have you got for me this time?" I know because that's what he always says. But he didn't finish saying it, because Pat began to bark. "Friend," I assured Pat. "Friend!"

Pat would have none of it. He went on barking and jumping up and down, straining at the leash until I thought he was going to pull my arm out of its socket. Habib, of course, got back in his car and stayed there, until finally I had to grab Pat by the collar and march him back to the Escort and lock him in, where he continued to bark and jump up and down. He did not like Habib. He did not like Rick Olsen, who arrived shortly thereafter. He did not like Bob Castle. All of a sudden he did not like anybody. It was obvious that there were far more people than he felt he could watch comfortably, and he'd rather just eat them all and forget the whole thing.

Apparently I was not doing a very good job of teaching Pat to be a police dog, though I didn't think he would really have bitten anybody.

As I headed back toward the door, Habib, now out of his car, inquired, "When did you turn lion tamer?"

"He's just a little ol' dog," I protested.

"Right," Habib said. "And King Kong was just a monkey, and the Titanic just took on a little water. Keep that animal away from me from now on."

"I will."

"What are you doing with a pit bull anyway?" he added.

"It was a stray," I said.

"So you had to keep it."

"Well—"

"How many cats? How many dogs? How many *kids,* even?"

"Now wait a minute," I objected, highly displeased at having my adopted children put in the same category with cats and dogs. Well, my adopted children, and Shane, and the two or three other street people, well, eight or ten or maybe more, whom I'd given temporary homes to before Shane, and—

"Never mind, never mind," Habib said resignedly. "The world would be a lot better place to live in if more people took in strays—human or otherwise. Just—like I said—keep it away from me. And that's what I'm supposed to decide whether or not it's dead?" Habib inquired, looking now at what was left of—presumably; we didn't have a formal identification yet—Helen Thorne. "Well, guess what, it's dead."

By that time Olsen and Castle, Castle with the search warrant allowing us to work the crime scene without the consent of the owner, had also arrived, and they were bustling around with photographs, measurements, collections, and so forth. Bob took careful scaled photos of the footprints, since it was going to be just about impossible to lift them intact, although he tried that too.

There was really far less to do here than there had been at the Huffman residence, because this was a public place. But even so it took long enough, and I was giving serious consideration to crawling in the back seat with the dog and sleeping until they got through—that would be after Habib left, *hmm*ing all the way—and I could get in there. But it was just as well I didn't because about four-forty-five another car pulled up in the alley, and a burly man in a white shirt and white pants got out. "What's going on here?" he demanded.

Millner turned and produced identification. "And who are you?"

"Leon Aristides. I'm head chef here." I'm not sure what I would have expected a head chef to look like—perhaps a little French, a little willowy—but Leon Aristides was about six-two and would probably have gone two hundred forty pounds. His chef's clothing was definitely not clean or fresh, and he didn't seem to have shaved in several days. I could easily imagine him as a short-order cook in a place that might be named "Bennie's." It was somewhat more difficult to imagine him in connection with French cuisine.

I couldn't tell whether Millner was wrestling with the same stereotypes or not, as he demanded, "Do you usually arrive this early?"

"Only on Sunday," Aristides replied. "Or did you think that Sunday brunch buffet prepared itself? My pastry cooks'll be here in another twenty minutes or so. What's it to you?"

"You might as well send them home," Millner said, "because there won't be any Sunday brunch buffet."

"The hell you say! We've got reservations for a party of fifty, besides all the drop-ins! And I've got a carload of vegetables and fruit—"

"Come 'ere," Millner said, and led him past the footprints, into the receiving area. The rough wooden door into the office was wide open, and Aristides blanched.

"That's Helen?" he demanded.

"I was going to ask you that," Millner said. "You need a closer look?"

"Shit, no," Aristides said. "That's Helen."

"You sure? You're close enough to see her face?"

"I don't need to be close enough to see her face."

"We need that for a formal identification."

Aristides told Millner what he could do with his formal identification, but of course Millner still insisted Aristides look at her face. "Now, let's have a formal identification. That's your employer?"

"Partner," Aristides said sullenly.

"Partner?"

"Helen Thorne. That's Helen Thorne. We bought this place together. But Helen is...Helen was...prettier than me. When are you going to be able to get her out of here?"

"Why?"

"Because I've still got reservations for a party of fifty. Look, I care, all right?" Aristides added. "But Helen and me were partners. That's all. Not even—quite—friends. Just partners. Helen knew business. I know how to cook. That's all. And—you gotta understand—when Helen and me opened up, I put every penny I had and then some into this place. And I got a family to take care of. Helen did all the front work. Helen—like I said—looked pretty. She talked nice. Me, all I can do is cook. I'm scared, okay? If we lose business—if *I* lose business now—it's all down the tubes. All of it. Whoever it was killed her, he didn't do me no favors. And—I got a party of fifty coming in.''

I wondered whether that party of fifty would show up, but of course it would: this had happened, or at least had been reported, too late to make the morning papers, and who gets up and listens to the radio, or watches the television news, before going out to brunch?

Millner probably had the authority to shut the place down anyway, but it was open to question whether he could make a shutdown work without calling the Board of Health. But the crime scene people were through, and Olsen called an ambulance crew to remove the body.

Without asking permission, Aristides telephoned his cleaning crew to come in *now* to attend to an unfortunate mess that had developed overnight. I couldn't help wondering what the cleaning crew was going to say—or do—when they found out exactly what the unfortunate mess that they were expected to clean up consisted of, but I didn't want to take the time to ponder that because, now that the scene had been vacated, I wanted to get in there fast.

There wasn't, on the surface, much to see that was in any way different from what I'd seen at the Huffmans'. Although it would take Habib to say for sure, and he probably wouldn't be saying anything until Monday, I was willing to bet that the same weapon, or at least an identical one, had been used. Helen was barely recognizable; Aristides had to have known her well to identify her so quickly. Computer fragments had spattered down over the blood and brain and bone and skull fragments on the concrete floor. For some reason, that seemed to be trying to trigger something in my mind, but I couldn't figure out what.

Apparently Helen had been on the same net as Harry and as Eric Huffman, because the same near-gibberish was on her printouts, on printouts that had been yanked out and thrown impatiently—or furiously—on the floor, and on printouts that were still sticking out of the printer. The numbers looked all right until examined closely—you really couldn't tell that "321" was supposed to be "432" until you checked the sums. But the letters, the words that were supposed to be explaining the numbers, were clearly garbled.

The fact that what seemed to be her newest printouts were doing the same thing suggested that she, unlike Harry and Eric Huffman, hadn't had any luck finding a "medicine" for this virus. She had, presumably, died very frustrated.

There were many things I needed to do about this murder. There was nothing I could do about it right now, except try to question Leon Aristides. Legally, of course, I could question Leon Aristides any time I wanted to, but equally legally, he could tell me he had no intention of talking with me, and than I had a choice between leaving meekly or arresting him as a material witness, which would certainly guarantee he would not cooperate with me at any time in the future.

Aristides was hauling corrugated boxes of strawberries, grapes, cantaloupe, and lettuce in from his car. I got out of his way. A couple more men, presumably pastry cooks, came in through the back door, identified themselves to Millner, bridled visibly at the bloody—though now corpseless—office, and then, at Aristides's yell, went on into the kitchen to make whatever it is pastry cooks at a place like Helen's Club make at five o'clock on a Sunday morning.

I told Millner I was going home, and I went.

Everybody else was still asleep except, of course, Cameron; even Pat had gone to sleep in the car and roused only long enough to get out of the car, curl up in front of his never-used dog house, and return to sleep. I went on and got Cameron out of his crib, changing him and putting a cute little jumpsuit on him. Then I gave him a bowl of fruit yogurt (on the hearth, not in the high chair), got him a small—a *very* small—glass of orange juice, checked to be sure that the doors were locked and there was nothing in the immediate vicinity likely to be harmed by him or harmful to him, and went to sleep on the couch.

Guess what? Cameron now knows how to unlock doors.

I woke up again at seven-thirty to find Pat indoors wagging his hindquarters extremely happily as Cameron fed Pat fruit yogurt with a spoon.

So I turned my back, pulled a sofa throw cushion over my head, and went right back to sleep. Why not? Cameron was happy. Pat was happy. They were both quiet. The yard is fenced.

I was *tired,* dammit.

Hal got up at eight-fifteen, which was cutting it close, considering he has church—half an hour away—starting at nine. I pretended to be asleep. He is seventeen—nearly eighteen, now—and should certainly be old enough to fend for himself at breakfast occasionally. He ate a bowl of cereal fairly quietly, took care to relock the front door behind himself, and left rather noisily, which is the pickup truck's fault, not his.

He did not, I noticed, evict Pat. Harry got up at nine and did that. Cameron, of course, howled.

There is a limit to how long, and under what conditions, I can pretend to be still asleep. I got up, washed Cameron, and went to think about breakfast for the rest of us.

I was tired of Cheerios. I was tired of muffins. There wasn't any bacon; I had quit buying it because neither Harry nor I needed the cholesterol or saturated fat. There was no sausage for the same reason. The eggs were there, but what are eggs with no sausage or bacon, besides inedible? No, I did *not* want to make biscuits.

The light dawned. Harry could take himself, me, and Cameron out to breakfast. Shane probably wouldn't wake up till noon anyway, and if he did get up while we were gone he could fend for himself, as Hal had done.

Harry could take us out to breakfast . . . at Helen's Club.

Provided, of course, that I artfully kept him from finding out why I wanted to go to Helen's Club.

Not artfully enough, or else he has me very well figured out. But after sufficient questioning to ensure that he knew exactly why I wanted to go there, he laughed and off we went.

On the way, Harry commented, "This seems to let Shane out. I mean, he wouldn't have any way of knowing this . . . Helen Thorne, or any reason—"

"He didn't have any reason on Huffman, either," I pointed out. "And he was out late last night."

"Do you really suspect him?" Harry asked.

"No," I said. "If I did, I wouldn't have him living with us, now would I?"

When we arrived at Helen's, Cameron's joy was evident. We've taken him out so many times he recognizes a restaurant—not just a restaurant we have been to, but the concept of *restaurant*. Restaurants are places where lots of people pay attention to him and bring him interesting things to eat, including red suckers, which I for some unaccountable (to him) reason won't buy for him.

Would I be accused of unspeakable vulgarity if I were to admit that I had a hearty appetite, and enjoyed breakfast very much? The contemplation of murder definitely was not sufficient to distract my attention from bacon, sausage, and ham, fried eggs, scrambled eggs, poached eggs, biscuits, muffins, cornbread, fresh fruit, hash browns, grits (this is, after all, still the South), cream gravy, butter, honey butter, and assorted little pastries that I didn't even have names for—all cooked by somebody who was not me. Ah, the calories, the cholesterol, and for once I didn't even care.

But after the meal, assuming that maybe at least some of the chefs and chef's helpers were now able to slow down a little, I left Harry and Cameron contemplating banana slices marinated in pineapple juice and sneaked back to the kitchen.

Leon Aristides was in the cleaned—*very* cleaned—office contemplating what looked like a payroll. "You mind if I see that?" I asked.

Obviously recognizing me from earlier in the morning, he shrugged and handed it over.

There was only one name on it I recognized, and the recognition came as a distinct shock. Shane Corbett had been employed by (I started to say "had

worked for") Helen's Club three whole days, and
then had been fired. "This Corbett," I said to Leon
Aristides, "is he the only person who's been fired in
the last few months?"

"Hired *or* fired," Aristides replied. "Laziest kid
I ever saw. We hired him as a busboy. He couldn't
even clear a table—that's *one* table, not six—without stopping to yack for fifteen minutes. In fifteen
minutes he ought to be able to clear half the tables
in the banquet room."

"Who fired him?"

"Me," Aristides said. "You're not thinking it was
him that killed Helen, are you?"

"I haven't picked anybody yet. I was just asking
questions."

"Well, don't pick him. He's lazy. He's stupid. But
he ain't dishonest and he ain't mean. He'd rather
beg than work, but from all I've seen I'd say he
wouldn't steal. And he took the firing okay. Just
said, 'Everybody fires me. Sure do wish I could figure out why.' I told him why, and he said, 'I was just
tryin' to be friendly.' You know what I think? I think
the kid thinks life is one big game of Dungeons and
Dragons. He told me one time he'd been living
mostly on the street for three years, and he sure had
met a lot of interesting people."

"Did he talk a lot about Dungeons and Dragons?" I asked.

"Oh, yeah," Aristides said. "For a couple of days
he had a running game set up in the storage room,

and every break time him and some of the other busboys would be out there playing.''

This bothered me. Dungeons and Dragons, like most fantasy role-playing games, attracts several different types of people. It attracts imaginative people, the kind that might someday be writing fantasy books of their own. It attracts teenagers. It attracts people who are bored with their real life and would much prefer to live in fantasy worlds.

It attracts my son Hal. It does not attract me.

And it attracts a goodly share of nuts and flakes, most of whom just go about their nutty and flaky way, but a few of whom commit suicide or kill. There'd been a case in the paper just a few months ago, I couldn't remember now where, in which an intelligent, creative teenage girl had been killed by another fantasy game player—one of the nut-and-flake variety—who had somehow convinced himself he had to really kill her to free her from her current role so that she could go on to another role in another game.

Of course I didn't just ask Aristides about Shane Corbett. I asked about many things. The restaurant's financial picture—sound, according to Aristides. Helen's love life—nonexistent, according to Aristides. Helen's relationship with Eric Huffman. "Never heard of him," said Aristides. Had she ever been involved with ham radio? Aristides said no, why would she have been? Helen's activity on computer nets?

"Oh, yeah, she used two or three different nets," Aristides said. "Used to get her stock market quotations and her news from computer nets. Used computers to pay some of the bills—had some way she could link into her bank's system or something like that and transfer money from her account into somebody else's account. She used computers a lot. She sure was mad when that virus got into the computer. I never seen her so mad. It screwed up all the accounts. Me, I don't use computers anyway, but I don't know what I'm going to do about the accounts. I guess I'll have to get somebody in here that knows about computers and can put it all back together. What do you think that'll cost me?"

"I haven't the slightest idea," I replied. "How long have you known Helen?"

"Me and her go way back," Aristides said. "Twenty years or so. We'd been planning for this place for a good fifteen years before we finally had the money to open up."

"Anything between you and her other than a business relationship?"

He laughed. "You gotta be kidding. I already told you *no*. Lady, I got a wife and five kids. Helen Thorne I don't need—that way."

"Is there any possibility she was, uh, attracted to other women?"

"No. I've seen her with men a lot. Just so far as I know, she didn't have anybody right now. That doesn't mean for sure she didn't. She could have had

somebody and I wouldn't have had any reason to
know about it. We were business partners. That's
all. I saw her here and nowhere else. And if she had
a beau, well, most likely she'd have taken him
somewhere else.''

"She'd have taken him?" I asked. That was a
rather odd choice of phrases.

"Let him take her," Aristides said. "But she'd
have decided. She was a Dragon Lady, she was. Now
mind you, that's not a put-down. She had to be a
Dragon Lady to make it in this business.''

When I got back out in front, Cameron was
asleep in his high chair and Harry was working a
crossword puzzle. That meant he was very, very
bored. Harry never works crossword puzzles.

I disentangled Cameron from the high chair (he
didn't wake up) and strapped him into his car seat
(he still didn't wake up—this was definitely his nap
time, and he didn't intend to give up that nap for
anybody or anything), then put myself into the front
seat and fastened my own seat belt. "Harry," I said,
"Helen Thorne's business partner says she belonged to several computer nets. Did you know
her?"

"I've been trying to figure out," Harry said. "I
think I encountered a Helen Thorne once or twice
on one of the computer nets, but I don't know if it
was this one or not. She never mentioned what she
did for a living and I didn't ask. I'm sure I never met
her face to face.''

"Do you think Eric might have known her?"

"If he did he never mentioned it to me. He probably knew her about as well as I did, which in effect is not at all."

I sat in the car and thought all the way home. What bothered me was this: Eric Huffman's computer had suffered from a virus. Eric Huffman had given Shane Corbett a place to live. Eric Huffman was dead.

Helen Thorne's computer had suffered from the same virus. Helen Thorne's restaurant had given Shane Corbett a job, until Leon Aristides fired him three days later. Helen Thorne was dead.

Harry Ralston's computer had suffered from the same virus. Harry Ralston had given Shane Corbett a place to live.

Now were we going to throw Shane Corbett out, or not?

Had Eric Huffman decided to evict Shane Corbett?

I was not happy. Definitely I was not happy.

I was even less happy when I mentioned this chain of thought to Harry and Harry laughed at me. "Several thousand computers in the Dallas-Fort Worth area caught the virus," he pointed out, "and if Shane's been on the street three years, quite a few people have evicted him or fired him. Now quit worrying. He's just a dumb-ass kid, that's all."

I hoped so. I surely did hope so.

SIX

WHEN I LEFT for work Monday morning, I still
hadn't decided what to do, or not do, about Shane.
I couldn't arrest him, because there wasn't enough
probable cause for a warrant. Besides that, my gut
feeling still agreed with Harry. But logic said that if
this was a coincidence—and in fact coincidences are
just as likely in police work as in anything else—it
still was a mighty big coincidence.

I hadn't asked Shane about Helen Thorne yet,
because I hadn't decided what to ask him. That
might have been stupid too, though, because I
wanted to ask him before he'd gotten the news in
other ways, and it would certainly be in the Monday paper. Would Shane read a newspaper? Perhaps not, but Harry certainly would, and if he then
left it lying around—as he always does—even Shane
would be likely to notice the headlines. Assuming,
of course, that he was literate. Come to think of it,
he had to be literate to play Dungeons and Dragons.

I had taken the opportunity, stealthily I hoped, to
investigate Shane's sneakers, which at the time I
decided to investigate them were residing under the
coffee table in the living room, Shane being at the

time still in bed. There was no blood on them, and they were not the same pattern, though they did seem to be about the same small-for-a-man size as the sneakers that had left the blood tracks on the concrete at the back of Helen's Club. To the best of my knowledge, Shane had no other sneakers.

To the best of my knowledge, Shane also did not have an ax or a way to get to Helen's Club and back.

And he had not dumped any bloody clothing on the floor, which, his habits being like Hal's habits, was his customary laundry basket.

On the face of things, it was impossible for Shane to have been the killer. This did not mean that I stopped worrying as I drove to work that Monday morning.

Dutch Van Flagg was at his desk, gloomily reading the contents of his in-basket. I *think* he was sneaking things into my basket until I came in, at which time he smoothly shifted to Wayne Carlsen's basket. That sort of evened things out, because of course I always sneak things into Nathan Drucker's basket. I think it's Nathan who sneaks things into Dutch's basket.

I read—or skimmed—the contents of my in-basket in a great hurry and then, Dutch having departed with car keys in hand, I initialed everything that needed initialing, kept only the few things that really pertained to me, and then, with malice aforethought, this time dropped everything into (back into?) Dutch's basket.

We play this game of musical in-baskets, but the truth is that if we actually *read* the total contents of our in-baskets every day we'd spend three hours or more a day just reading, and that is not what we're paid to do.

One of the things we are paid to do is talk with witnesses. This time one of the witnesses was at my house, but I was darned if I was going to talk with him on my own time. I do too much on my own time anyway. Even if I wasn't aware of that fact, Harry would see to it that I was made aware of it. Frequently.

All right. Plan the day.

That, of course, is a joke. No matter how well and efficiently I plan my day, any joker who wants to can quickly unplan it with a gun or a knife or an ax. But I'd try to plan it anyway. So let's see. Go back and talk with Mrs. Huffman about Shane, about everything and everybody else I could think of that could in any imaginable way connect to the crime.

Then go talk with Shane, at whatever length seemed at that moment to be called for.

What next? Well, that might depend on what I got from Shane. But tentatively, return to Helen's Club to talk to any chefs, chef's assistants, busboys, and so forth who weren't in on Sunday.

Maybe I'd also better take along a fingerprint kit and get elimination prints wherever they seemed called for. That, of course, meant calling Irene and asking what elimination prints we needed.

What first?

That was obvious, as it had been obvious for several weeks. I called Methodist Hospital to check on Lori. "She's just the same," Donna told me, sounding bone weary.

"Hal said she seemed restless—'wiggly' was his word—several times over the weekend. And she seemed a little restless last time I was there. Have the doctors said anything?"

Donna semi-laughed, sounding more hysterical than amused. "You know doctors never say anything. Are you coming in tonight?"

"I hope so. But they've got me on this murder thing—"

"That's so crazy," Donna interrupted. "You're Major Case Squad, not Homicide. Why do they keep giving you murders?"

"I don't really get that many," I answered. "Maybe three or four a year, and then only when they look really *strange* in some way. Like right now I'm on these ax murders."

"Oh? I didn't realize you'd gotten that. How do they look?"

"Weird," I said. "There is just nothing to go on."

"You'll think of something." Donna did not sound at all interested. I could well believe that; she had too much else to think about. But she did, out of politeness, ask me what was going on and I told her this and that, which was not much. "I wouldn't swap jobs with you," she told me. "Look, I've got to go now, the doctor's here and I want to try to talk with him.''

"I guess it's back to the salt mines for me," I said tritely. "Take care of yourself."

"Yeah," she said, and I heard her phone clatter back down before I had a chance to hang up.

All right, now what? If I rearranged my day a little bit I could manage, just by coincidence, mind you, to be at home talking to Shane just at lunchtime, which would mean I could have lunch at home, which would be convenient. But to do that, naturally, I needed to do something else first, and I had talked with Clara Huffman about all I needed to right now. It was obvious that whatever I asked her, she was going to try to convince me that Shane was the killer, in which supposition I was not a hundred percent certain she was wrong, but I certainly was not convinced that she was right. But for now...

The problem was that I kept having this nagging feeling that there was something we had missed at Helen's, something that somebody should have spotted and nobody did, and I was talking to myself about everything else under the sun to avoid that feeling, because all the ident people become very bent out of shape at any suggestion they might have missed something at a crime scene. To be sure, insulting Bob Castle that way was not as much lèse-majesté as insulting Irene Loukas that way, but still it would cause hard feelings that would continue until and unless I really did find something, at which time there would be tremendous shouting and sulking downstairs in the ident section.

After arguing with myself a while longer, I decided I couldn't get away with stalling till lunchtime. I took off for home, so I could get this business of questioning Shane out of the way and then figure out what to do about that feeling. That was the intention. As usual, things didn't work out as I had intended; this time, it was mainly because I couldn't find Shane. I asked Harry his location. "Gone," Harry said laconically.

"What do you mean, gone?"

"I mean gone. He took off. I thought at first he'd only taken off for a few hours, until I looked in Cameron's room for my best screwdriver" (he did not have to explain to me why it was necessary to look in Cameron's room for a screwdriver; Cameron had been teething on screwdrivers) "and I found all his stuff gone. Like I said, he took off."

"Took off where?" I demanded.

"How should I know? When he left I just thought he was going job hunting again, so I didn't ask. And even if I had, I very much doubt he'd have told the truth."

That was probably true, but... "You didn't even let me know? I mean, when you did find out?"

"I tried to call your office, and you'd left. Dispatch said you were out on something and they probably couldn't get you by radio. I tried to call

Captain Millner, and he was out of pocket too. What was I supposed to do, Deb? He was already gone."

I didn't know what he was supposed to do. I did know that if a drifter like Shane vanishes he can stay vanished a very long time—like permanently—and although Shane wasn't, at least in my opinion, a very good suspect on two murders, the fact remained he was all the suspect we had.

So I called dispatch, and dispatch, wise in the ways of where people trying to get out of Fort Worth are likely to be hitchhiking, put it on the air, and exactly twenty minutes later Shane, complete with backpack et cetera, was delivered back to my front door by a police car.

To say that he was unhappy might possibly be an understatement. To say that *I* was unhappy definitely was not an understatement.

"You didn't have to bring me back like this," Shane was protesting, as he came in the front door. "I haven't done anything! I mean, I was just leaving because I was in the way here and all, with Hal worried about this Lori of his and Deb was busy and Harry was busy all the time and I figured if I just got out of the way it would help, and nobody told me not to..."

He came to a halt, looking at me. "Shane," I said, "I distinctly remember telling you that you had a choice between staying with me or going to jail."

"Yeah, but that was a while ago."

"It wasn't that long a while ago. Now, would you like to tell me why you took off like that?"

Dead silence.

"You need me to stick around?" the patrolman asked me.

"No, thanks," I replied absently. The patrolman left. Harry picked up, then put down, a copy of *Soldier of Fortune* magazine. Cameron, who had decided to take a brief nap under the dining room table, rolled over, sighed, and reinserted his thumb in his mouth. The silence continued.

Then, abruptly, Shane got tired of the silence. "I told you. Everybody was busy and I was in the way and—"

"Bullshit," I said loudly.

Shane looked shocked. Harry, who has known me a lot longer than Shane has, did not look shocked. Cameron, of course, was still asleep.

"Now tell me the truth," I said.

Dead silence again. I kept waiting.

"Well, it was this way," Shane said finally, and stopped again.

"It was what way?" I had no intention of helping him out this time. I'd helped him out all I wanted to and then some.

"There was this place I used to work."

"Helen's?"

"Yeah. Helen's. And they owed me for those three days because they hadn't paid me, and this guy, this Leon, he was gonna pay me, and he told me to drop by Saturday night and he'd give me a check."

"I thought you had a date Saturday night."

"Well, I did. This was after the date."

"How'd you get over there?" I asked.

"This girl I was with, she said she'd take me over there. We figured if I got paid then we could, you know, go do something, you know. So she took me over there."

"What was this girl's name?"

"I don't know. I met her at, like, you know, this place."

"No, I do *not* know that place," I said distinctly. *"What* place?"

After considerable more prodding, I finally was able to ascertain with a fair degree of certainty that Shane had met the girl—whose name he clearly really did not know—in some kind of honky-tonk, juke joint, or whatever you call them today, on a side street off Belknap. They'd done some drinking, gone through most of the money she had, taken off somewhere else, and then decided to go over to Helen's and pick up Shane's check, which they would then try to cash at a liquor store, probably picking up a bottle or two at the same time.

But they didn't get the check. And what Shane claimed to have seen at Helen's would do a pretty fair job of sobering up the town drunk.

"What time was this?" I asked. "When you got to Helen's, I mean."

"I guess about sometime after midnight, because we went to this movie, see, after we left the bar" (I doubted that but did not say so) "and it didn't let out until after midnight and then we went right on over there."

"To Helen's?"

"Yeah. The front was all closed up, but I figured there'd still be people in the back working. So I got this girl, Lindy, I think that was her name, Lindy, to drive me around the back, and I got out of the car, and the back door was standing open, so I went in and there was this...this...*person* there and he came running at me with this *ax* thingie and it was all bloody and I ran away and got back in the car and we left. But—"

"Was this person a man or woman?" I interrupted.

"Danged if I could tell," he said. "He—I mean whoever, he or she—was wearing this yellow raincoat thing and had it pulled up over his head and he or she or whatever had on these sneakers, and the raincoat and sneakers were bloody too like the ax, and I'm telling you, he was chasing me with that ax, he chased me back out into the alley and I got in the car and slammed the door and this girl, she pulled out as fast as she could and the person with the ax was like chasing us up the alley, I mean it was like *Friday the Thirteenth* or something."

"And this happened Saturday night."

"Yeah."

"So on Monday morning you decide to leave Fort Worth."

"Yeah."

"How come?"

He stared at me. "Because I was *scared,* man!"

When Hal calls me *man* I reply, "I'm not a man, I'm your mother." I was somewhat pleased that I was not Shane's mother, so I forbore to point out that I also was not a man. Instead I asked, "If you got scared Saturday night, how come you waited to leave until Monday morning?"

I watched Shane look over at Harry, who was a silent witness. "You know that phone call I got this morning? The one you answered and it was for me?"

"You mean the one where the caller sounded funny?" Harry said. "Or the one where they didn't want to hire you back?"

"The one where the caller sounded funny," Shane said.

"Yeah, I remember," Harry said. "What about it?"

"Well, it was a person, I couldn't tell if it was a guy or a girl, and it said . . . it said it was gonna kill me too."

"Rrright," I said dubiously.

"Hey, man, I'm not lying!" Shane protested. "This voice, I mean it was all scratchy and all, this voice said if I told anything they were gonna come and kill me too, just like they killed Ms. Thorne with this ax, just like they did Eric, and man, I don't want to get killed with no ax!''

The whole thing sounded maximum unlikely to me—for one thing, how was this hypothetical person in the yellow raincoat going to know Shane was at my house? But for all I know Shane might have told forty people, each of whom could have told forty other people (assuming, of course, that the whereabouts of Shane Corbett was of general interest, which I found it fairly reasonable to assume it was not).

There was always the possibility he was telling the truth...and suddenly I had a good idea what it was that had been nagging at me all morning, that feeling of something that needed to be done.

Telling Shane that if he didn't stay put this time I would definitely see to it he spent the next few weeks in jail as a material witness, which if I had bat-ass sense he'd be doing anyway, I went out the door, got back into the police car that had been assigned to me, and headed back out onto Camp Bowie Boulevard.

Helen's was not open yet. I'd already noticed the sign that said it opened at eleven weekdays, and even though it wasn't yet ten-thirty, I was sure that Leon Aristides was there, probably along with many if not most of his helpers. In fact, come to think of it, probably just about everybody except the service people would be there. The problem was that I didn't really want to talk with any of them, but I was sure they—or at least somebody, most likely Leon Aristides, as he was now the owner—would be a little perturbed if they found me prowling around in their alley without telling them first.

And that, quite suddenly and for no apparent reason, brought on another question that I should have asked before I left the police station, let alone the house—a question so urgent, in fact, that I pulled over at the next 7-Eleven to use a pay phone.

Irene Loukas answered, which meant I was going to get yelled at no matter what the answer to the question was. Meekly, I asked it anyway. "Did anybody check the Dumpster at Helen's Club?"

"They should have," Irene answered. She considers that no crime scene is worked adequately unless she works it herself, but some hours in her day are required for sleeping, eating, and other necessary functions.

"I know they should have; what I want to know is whether they did." By phrasing the question that way I was throwing Bob to the wolves—there is a word for a female wolf, but I'm not going to use it, even though I suspect Irene would take it as a compliment—if in fact he hadn't checked the Dumpster. But after all, I really did have to know. If somebody else had checked the Dumpster that might mean I didn't have to do it, though in view of Shane's information (if it was true) I probably had to anyway.

All of which is to say that I knew what I was looking for. It's just that it took me a little while to realize that it might be in the Dumpster. If I was lucky, somebody had already searched the Dumpster and found no evidence in it.

If I wasn't lucky...

My luck was out. "Let me check." The tone of her voice was distinctly unfriendly. It was even less friendly when she returned a minute later to inform me, very reluctantly, that the Dumpster had not been checked.

I would have been much happier, even if she had yelled at me, if the answer had been different. Because that meant guess who was going to get to check the Dumpster?

Back in the days when I first started policing, my mother used to worry herself into a tailspin about the possibility of my getting shot. I told her once that if she really had to worry about something she should worry about something more likely, like maybe the possibility of my getting gangrene or something like that as a result of digging into somebody else's garbage. She didn't believe me, even when I explained further. But the problem is that every crime scene has a getaway route, and many, many criminals discard things along that route.

I remember one of the first robberies I worked. This fellow had entered a real estate office, wearing a wool ski mask in July in Fort Worth, and demanded all the money. Of course all he got was petty cash—I can't imagine what he *expected* to get—but he did manage to frighten people quite a lot. Someone saw him leave, and someone else saw the direction he was going, and the dispatchers kept telling us all about the ski mask, as if he were still going to be wearing it all over town.

As it happened, I found the ski mask right in the middle of a broadcast (and right in the middle of an alley, for that matter) and got on the radio to interrupt the dispatcher. "Cancel the ski mask. Subject is *not* wearing a ski mask. Repeat, subject is *not* wearing a ski mask."

One of the dispatchers inquired, somewhat tartly, just what I meant by that, but he sounded mollified when I explained that the subject could not be wearing the ski mask because I was holding it in my hand at that very moment.

Sometimes objects, like the ski mask, are simply discarded on the escape route. But just as often—especially if the subject hopes to keep the escape route a secret—things are thrust into Dumpsters and garbage cans along the route. And this, as I indicated, means that police—especially lower-echelon police—get to spend a lot of time with their hands in other people's garbage. This, pre-AIDS, was at least a little less nerve-wracking than it is now.

I stopped at a drugstore to buy plastic gloves, the kind that are sold for people to use while washing dishes. Not that they were going to do a whole lot of good, because it was pretty obvious that the only way I was going to do a decent job of inspecting the Dumpster behind Helen's Club was to get into the Dumpster, a task I did not relish at all.

At least I had worn washable clothing today, which wasn't always the case.

Need I say that when I stopped at the back of the restaurant to tell Leon Aristides what I was doing, he grinned wryly and said, "Glad it's you and not me." Neither of us mentioned the peels and other scraps from the crates of fruits and vegetables he had brought in early Sunday morning; neither of us mentioned the garbage and leftovers that, in less enlightened (or less wasteful) ages, would have been used to fatten a few pigs for slaughter.

I do not enjoy crawling into a Dumpster. I do not enjoy telling anybody I am going to crawl into a Dumpster. I do not enjoy explaining to anybody what I happen to see or otherwise encounter while I am in a Dumpster. Suffice it to say that I found nothing at all in the Dumpster that seemed in any way related to our investigation, including no yellow raincoats, bloody sneakers (white), or axes, and by the time I got out of the Dumpster I was definitely due if not overdue for a bath. That did not, however, mean I was going to get one right now. I still had more alley searching to do.

At least nobody was likely to bother me. Nobody was likely to want to get close enough to disturb me in any way.

I walked up the alley one way. I walked back down it, past the back of the restaurant, and down to the other end of the block, then headed back up. Of course, I had covered all this distance the night of the murder, with the assistance of my pit bull, Pat. Of course, Bob Castle had—probably—covered it all again on Sunday, in the daylight. This still did not mean something could not have been missed.

Something had been.

At the back of the alley, in a little thicket of wild plum that had grown up right here in the heart of the city adjacent to the back of what had once been a house and garage and was now a sign-painting establishment, was a brown paper grocery bag, with some abandoned trash spilling out of the top of it.

There was no reason to investigate the waxed paper and banana peel that suggested—were probably meant to suggest—that this had been somebody's lunch, but this bag was far too large to have held only that lunch. Furthermore, this bag had not been rained on, had not been dried out and weathered by the Fort Worth sun. This bag was fresh; it could not, in my opinion, have lain here longer than about two days. Which put it exactly in the period under question.

I decided to be cautious. If the bag did turn out to be only somebody's lunch debris, I would have wasted a couple of (all right, a few) negatives on a roll of film, a little time spent measuring. But if, as

I suspected, this was somewhat more than it appeared to be at a glance, its exact position was likely to become a subject of courtroom discussion, a discussion that could prove acrimonious if I didn't know the *exact* location et cetera.

I moved the police car, which I had left at the back of Helen's, on down and parked it beside the clump of wild plum. (This, of course, was after I had made sure there were no tire tracks or footprints to be seen.) I got the camera out and photographed the bag from the front, from the left side, from the right side, and from directly above; the trees and the back wall of the sign place prevented me from getting behind it.

That done, I paced off the distance to the corner where the alley joined onto the side street and measured the distance from the back right corner of the garage. That gave me a triangulation from two fixed points; I could now explain exactly where I had found the bag.

I got out a large plastic evidence bag from the trunk and then thought better of it; if, as I hoped, there was something in the paper bag that had blood on it, sealing it into a plastic bag would cause it to rot. So I did not dump the paper bag into the plastic bag; instead, I dumped its contents out onto the plastic bag ... and hit pay dirt.

One yellow slicker, fairly high quality, the kind that has a layer of what looks like plastic fused to a layer of what looks like heavy cloth, canvas or something like that. The kind used by police, fire fighters, long-distance truckers, anybody who has to be out in the weather a lot. And one pair of old white sneakers, the kind that somebody probably bought at K-Mart or one of its clones. The condition of both items made it easy to assume that somebody had worn them to slaughter hogs or to commit an ax murder, and there hadn't been any hog slaughtering going on in this part of Fort Worth in the living memory of anybody but the oldest residents.

The two were wrapped around not an ax, which certainly wouldn't fit into a paper grocery bag, but around a hatchet, which would. It was reasonable to assume that Shane might not know the difference between an ax and a hatchet.

I didn't even have to wonder about where the hatchet had come from. Stenciled on the handle was one word: HUFFMAN.

The chances that Helen had been the victim of a copycat killer had now shrunk to about one in ten thousand.

Unfortunately, I was no closer than I ever had been to figuring out who, besides Shane Corbett, had come into close and unhappy contact with both Eric Huffman and Helen Thorne.

And, of far less importance to everybody but me, I had abruptly become a good bit farther from a bath.

I picked up my walkie-talkie from where it lay on the car seat, keyed my mike, and asked dispatch to get somebody from ident out here.

"YOU STINK," Irene informed me.

"No shit, Sherlock."

"What've you been doing, Dumpster diving?"

"Got it on one."

"That's what I figured." The amenities having been observed, Irene turned her attention to my discovery. She had recently been promoted to head of the identification/crime scene section, and the expression on her face did not bode well for Bob Castle when he reported in this afternoon. I would have felt a lot more sympathetic if I hadn't been the one to have to do the Dumpster diving Bob should have done and didn't.

The blood on the slicker wasn't quite dry yet, which meant that Irene could not yet use finger-print powder. But she turned the material this way and that, getting the light from both the sun and her powerful flashlight on it from multiple angles, hunting for patent prints—that is, fingerprints that had been made with blood and were therefore visible without developing. There were none.

Of course, there were no fingerprints on the sneakers.

The bag, with its other contents—after all, the lunch debris *could* have been the murderer's lunch—would all go into her office, there to be fingerprinted and otherwise examined at considerable length. Most of the work, I suspected, would be done by Bob Castle, under Irene's eye. Not that Irene couldn't do it herself; in fact, probably she would rather do it herself. But she would also consider it essential for Bob to be made sufficiently aware of his delinquencies in the matter of the Dumpster and the alley.

I turned the exposed roll of film over to Irene, got a new roll in exchange, and departed (sitting on a plastic bag I'd thrown over the seat) for home, where I intended to bathe before I even thought about talking to Shane again.

This time Shane was at home; it was Harry who had taken off.

I didn't, of course, know that at once; all I could tell was that the house was shut up, the pickup truck was gone, and the dog was in the front yard, where he was not supposed to be until after the mail had been delivered. But it was one-fifteen, so maybe the mail had already come. I certainly hoped so. The mail carrier made it clear, last time, that any time the dog was visible the mail would not be delivered. Not that I could blame her too much for that sentiment, although in fact Pat got along with mail carriers just fine until after the day a substitute mail carrier, not realizing he was only being greeted, sprayed Pat in the face with a can of Mace. This, unfortunately, left Pat with a permanent dislike for anybody in uniform, including mail carriers, UPS delivery people, and police officers.

When I unlocked the dead bolt, which we had gotten before we got the pit bull, I heard a scurry in the hall. "Who's there?" Shane yelled from somewhere in the back of the house.

"Just me," I replied, and he came out holding Cameron.

"I was afraid it was somebody else," he said. He scarcely needed to say he was afraid; the look on his face said it for him. But of whom, I wondered, was he afraid? Had he really gotten the phone call he said he'd gotten? Had he really seen an androgynous figure in a yellow slicker who chased him with a hatchet?

Or had he worn the yellow slicker and sneakers, carried the hatchet, himself?

But then I reminded myself that I knew he really had gotten the telephone call, because it was Harry, not Shane, who had answered the phone. But that did not mean the caller was who Shane said it was, or said what Shane said he said.

Maybe I was getting paranoid.

"Where's Harry?" I asked.

Definitely I was getting paranoid. I knew that for sure, as soon as Shane replied, "Oh, he said he had to go to the library and look up some stuff for that course he's taking. Hey, what's somebody his age doing still going to school? Me, I just couldn't wait to get old enough to where they'd let me drop out."

"Right," I thought, "and that's what you're do-ing jobless and mooching on other people, instead of out taking care of yourself." But that wasn't re-ally necessarily true; with the economy in the state it's in, many perfectly normal, appropriately edu-cated people are job hunting, and some of them, out of sheer desperation, wind up living with other people on just about the same basis as Shane.

But I wasn't interested in why Shane Corbett had dropped out of high school. I was interested in why Harry had seen fit to take off and leave Cameron in the care of Shane Corbett. It sounded maximum ir-responsible to me.

But I certainly wasn't going to ask Shane that.

And despite my paranoia, I wasn't going to search the house for Harry's chopped-up remains. I con-sidered it most unlikely (Ed Gough, if you remem-ber Ed Gough, notwithstanding) that Shane had been simultaneously committing murder and wax-ing the kitchen floor.

I had suddenly become aware that there was a strong odor of floor wax in the air—strong enough even to drown out my scent of garbage—and I asked about that, though I had a pretty good idea. "Oh, I've been waxing the kitchen floor," Shane told me, "to sort of apologize for being such a jerk and causing so much trouble. Hey, what's that funny smell? It's sort of like, well, like this time, one time, when I didn't have a place to stay and it, like, you know, started hailing and so I climbed into this, like, Dumpster.''

I know when I'm defeated. I went to take a bath.

SEVEN

I WAS STILL on duty, despite the bath. Detectives having to depart to bathe in the middle of their tour of duty, though not what you'd want to call common, is not totally unheard-of. This meant that I had to return to work, wet hair in December notwithstanding, unless I took the extra time required to blow-dry it, which I was not strongly inclined to do. I could not possibly take off leaving Shane to babysit Cameron, however, and this evening I was going to have some words—not very friendly and charming words—with Harry on the subject of *his* leaving Shane to babysit Cameron.

But I also could not take Cameron with me while I went to question witnesses. It is neither uncommon nor unheard-of for a detective, peacefully starting out to question witnesses, to wind up in a high-speed chase or even a shootout with somebody nobody ever heard of before the chase or the shootout started.

That left May Rector, the neighbor who'd last year asked me—as a favor to her, mind you—to allow her to watch Cameron any time Harry and I both had to be busy. We had finally managed to talk her into letting us pay her, but I still felt funny about the whole thing at times, especially when I remembered her indignant protest, "But you wouldn't want to deprive me of a blessing!"

But lately Harry had generally been home when I wasn't, especially in the daytime, and I wasn't sure what May—Sister Rector, as she had originally asked me to call her, before we turned by degrees into May and Deb—had as a daytime schedule. If she wasn't home I literally did not know what I was going to do, except maybe call Captain Millner and try to fast-talk myself into some comp time, of which I had weeks and weeks built up because just about every time I tried to take it Captain Millner would inform me, angrily or condescendingly depending on his mood, that while he was all for my taking comp time, *now* was not the right day to do it.

I could, of course, try to call Harry at the library, but that would depend on first, figuring out which library he was at; second, persuading the librarians there was really a good reason for somebody to go looking for him; third, explaining *why* I didn't want Cameron left with Shane (look, Cameron is my baby and Shane is possibly an ax murderer; do I really have to explain further? or at all, considering Shane would certainly be within earshot?); and fourth, waiting around while Harry came home, a project likely to take at least an hour and maybe more depending on how much puttering he found unavoidable on the way home.

I called May Rector. Then I gathered up Cameron, the diaper bag, the bottles he insists that, no matter what the pediatrician says, he is *not* old enough to do without, and a couple of bananas in case Sister Rector didn't have any, and I headed for the door.

"Hey, where are you going?" Shane demanded, trotting through the house with the vacuum cleaner in his hands and the dog right behind him.

"Back to work."

"With the *baby?*"

"I'm taking him to the babysitter."

Shane put on a tremendous show of being hurt. "But I can babysit him!"

"You are too busy with other things," I said brusquely. All right, I didn't say it very brusquely; even if Shane was possibly (but not probably) an ax murderer, that was no reason to hurt his feelings, and he really was working hard. I couldn't remember the last time the kitchen floor had gotten waxed. In this family, who has time? (Well, actually, Harry does right now, but catch him doing it.)

I did wonder how long it was going to take the floor to dry; Shane had applied the wax somewhat more liberally than the label directed.

Anyhow, I finally managed to leave first my home and then May's. Cameron hardly noticed my second departure, as he was busy chasing a large, long-haired cat that showed somewhat more inclination to allow itself to be mauled than either our calico,

Margaret Scratcher, or our recently adopted long-haired cat, Rags.

I drove toward town, meditating on Rags. She is the first long-haired cat I have ever owned. Owning her was not deliberate on my part. Someone abandoned her in my neighborhood, and there is a limit to how long I can allow a starving animal to meow or bark at my door before I take said animal in and feed it.

In the case of a long-haired animal, brushing also is necessary. It took six weeks, off and on as I had time, to brush Rags completely. Rags did not enjoy the process. Neither did I. In the course of it I completely filled ten large plastic grocery bags with wads of fur. Several times when the wad finally came loose, accompanied with tremendous meowings and scratchings on Rag's part and yelps and muttered curses on my part, so did such a shower of dandruff that I could only conclude that nobody had combed this cat since the day she was born. The vet concluded the cat was just over one year old.

Free cats, like free dogs, are expensive. Spaying, shots, cat food and litter because Margaret Scratcher refused to share, new booster shots for Margaret just in case Rags had brought in some germ to which Margaret's immunity had diminished... But she (Rags, I mean) does purr nicely, much better than Margaret, who is rather purr-deficient; and furthermore, I find that petting a long-haired cat provides many of the advantages of having a fur coat without any of the opprobrium.

All the same, I'd like to get my hands on those people—*any* of those people—who keep abandoning cats and dogs in the country on the grounds that the animals can take care of themselves. In the first place, the animals can't, and in the second place, even if they could they would do so only in manners that would become at the very least inconvenient, and quite possibly dangerous, to human beings.

Then I started wondering why I was thinking about Rags in the middle of a murder investigation, and concluded I was really thinking about Shane. Was he originally—because I knew now he'd been on the street since he was sixteen—a runaway kid, or a throwaway kid? And how many other Shanes, male and female, most of them younger and less charming than this one, were on the streets?

How many of them would someone bring in and feed and brush, and how many would be left, like so many stray dogs and cats, on the streets to starve?

How many of those brought in, fed, and brushed would turn and rend their benefactors rather as Rags had clawed me for brushing her, because by now they resented and distrusted the world?

Was that what Shane had done?

Logic went on insisting there was literally nobody else with any connection to both victims. But logic notwithstanding, I saw no signs of either resentment or distrust in Shane. And I could not, absolutely could not, believe that anybody could have committed those two ax murders and shown no signs at all of resentment or distrust to the world.

So meditating, I stopped the car rather unhappily in front of Clara Huffman's house. I was sorry as I could be for Clara Huffman, but damn it, I did not *like* the woman. She was just such a wishy-washy wimp. I had been hoping all the way across town that Mardee Hamilton would still be there; she was so much more sensible.

Mardee's car was there, so presumably Mardee also was there.

She was, and as she opened the door she did not look overwhelmingly happy to see me again. "Sorry," I said.

Mardee grimaced. "Was it that obvious?"

"It was that obvious."

"Then *I'm* sorry. It's not you so much as it is the whole idea of the police. I just got her halfway settled down and now you're going to set her off again. Oh, I know, you can't help it, but still ... Well, you might as well come in."

Actually, I had been getting a little tired of standing on the doorstep, but I hadn't been going to say anything about that quite yet.

There was a subtle, but noticeable, difference between the living room as it was now and the living room as I had last seen it. A small difference to be sure; the same overstuffed furniture was there, the same too-dark, too-heavy draperies were there, but the draperies were drawn back to let light in, the furniture had been rearranged just a little bit to make it more like a place where people might live and less like a furniture showcase. Clara was there, looking dreary, as she had every right to do, but the flowers on the end tables seemed—again more subtly than explicitly—cheerful rather than funereal.

Mardee's eyes didn't match the air of cheerfulness, which clearly she rather than Clara had imposed, and again I wondered whether, sexual orientation notwithstanding, Mardee Hamilton had been at least partially in love with her employer.

Clara stared at me. "Do I know you?" she demanded. "Yes, I think I know you. You're that policewoman. What do you want now?"

"I need to talk with you about—"

"Have you arrested that awful boy yet? That Shane? Have you arrested him?"

"Probable cause," Mardee said, halfway under her breath, and Clara rounded on her furiously.

"I don't know about things like that," Clara said. "Just, that awful boy killed my husband and nobody's doing anything about it."

Mardee sat down on the arm of a chair and tapped her fingertips impatiently on the corner of the end table beside it. "They're doing what they can, Clara," she said. "And nobody knows who killed Eric yet. It might have been the boy, but it might not have been. Now, why don't you let Detective Ralston ask her questions, so that she can leave? I'm sure she has other people she needs to talk with beside us."

"Not *us*," Clara said. "This is my house. Not yours."

"Of course it's yours," Mardee agreed. "I wouldn't have it if it came complete with a barrel of lollipops. There's too much *stuff* in it."

"They are my things and I like them."

"Fine. Like them all you want to. Just don't accuse me of wanting them."

"I wasn't accusing you—"

"Mrs. Huffman, Ms. Hamilton," I interrupted, "you guys can quarrel all you want to later, but right now I want to get some information."

Both Mardee and Clara looked at me with what appeared to be considerable amazement. Then Mardee broke into a light, and delighted, chuckle. Clara Huffman was not similarly amused, but she did nod sourly and say, "Go ahead."

I sat, uninvited, and asked, "Do you remember telling me about an ax you vaguely remembered seeing around the house?"

"It was in the den."

"I thought you said it was in Eric's study."

"Maybe it was in Eric's study."

"Where was it usually kept? With the woodpile?" I'd noticed a large woodpile at one side of the house, and though I don't think axes are usually kept with the woodpile that question was at least a starting point.

"No. We bought our firewood already cut."

"I thought you told me Eric used the ax to cut the firewood?"

"Well, he did, sometimes, when it was too long. But it came already cut."

"All right, where was the ax usually kept?" I asked, trying to sound more patient than I felt.

Dead silence.

Finally it was Mardee, restlessly detaching herself from the arm of the chair and moving to sit in, not on, another chair, who answered, "Can't you tell she doesn't know? Anything like that, Eric did it, and Clara had—has—less than no interest. I don't know where it has been kept lately; it was in the motor home until Eric got rid of it, the motor home I mean, but when he got the stuff out of the motor home I haven't the faintest idea where he put it. My guess would be that it was somewhere in the garage, but that's strictly a guess. And probably Clara did see the ax—by the way, it's a hatchet, not an ax—in the den occasionally, because I've seen Eric use it to kind of shave wood so that it would catch fire better. As to it being in Eric's study..." She shook her head.

"Are you sure you saw it there?" I asked Clara.

"I'm not sure of anything."

That I could well believe. "What did it look like?" I asked Mardee.

"Just a hatchet. Rather good quality. He stenciled his name on the handle of it so that it wouldn't get mixed up with somebody else's, when he went places where he might be using it outside and other people might be doing the same thing. Just in case you wonder; yes, I've been with him and Clara on weekend outings sometimes."

"And with him, just him, on other weekend outings," Clara said, in a rather expressionless tone of voice.

"Really, Clara," Mardee said, her voice light and amused. "You were the one who decided not to go."

"I didn't want to go. That didn't make it all right for you to go in my place."

"I went in my own place, not in your place." Mardee's voice was still light and amused, but rather more determinedly so. She got out a cigarette package and a lighter, and began to light a cigarette, more restlessly than out of any apparent need to smoke. In one part of my mind I began to wonder whether I might not have been too hasty in eliminating Mardee from suspicion; in another part of my mind, I began to wonder whether I might not have been too hasty in eliminating Clara from suspicion, and if so whether Mardee might not be our next victim; and in a third part of my mind I was wondering whether the jealousy Clara was exhibiting might have found another, perhaps more valid, target.

"Do you know Helen Thorne?" I asked abruptly, deliberately giving no signal as to which of the women I was aiming the question at.

"Who's that?" Clara demanded, in such a querulous, slightly confused old-lady voice that I wondered, suspiciously, whether it was put on.

"If you mean the Helen Thorne who ran Helen's Club, surely you know she's dead," Mardee replied at once.

"I knew. I wasn't sure you knew," I replied, and moved my head a little away from the stream of smoke.

"Does that bother you?" Mardee asked at once. "Sorry, I'll put it out."

"You know it bothers me," Clara said, "and you lit it anyway."

"Pardon me for living, Clara. You smoked yourself for twenty-five years."

"That was before Eric got his heart condition."

"True, true. All right, it's out, happy?"

"Why don't you just go home? I don't need you here anymore."

"If I could be a hundred percent sure you wouldn't be out in the car as soon as I was gone, I'd do exactly that."

"I'm a perfectly good driver."

"Yes, Miss Daisy, ma'am."

"What?" Clara said, as I tried not to chuckle.

"Clara, you're not a good driver when you're taking Xanax. Nobody is."

Xanax, I thought, and mentally shuddered. No wonder she's acting as if she's not exactly quite all here. I'd forgotten the Xanax.

"Anyway, why do *you* care?" Clara added spitefully. "There's nothing here for you anymore."

Very deliberately, Mardee lit another cigarette, blew smoke in Clara's direction, and put the cigarette out. "There never was anything here for me. But that doesn't mean I have the right to let you get out on the highway and kill innocent people."

"I don't need you anyway. I don't see why Eric said I did."

I had a feeling there was something pertinent that I wasn't being told. My expression must have communicated that impression to Mardee, because she lit a third cigarette. "Sorry," she said to me, "but this hogwash is getting to me. Believe me, Clara, if I had had any reason at all to suspect Eric was going to set up his will that way, I would have seen to it that he did not." She looked back at me again, carefully holding the cigarette so that the smoke went toward Clara instead of me.

"Do you remember that will I told you about?" she asked me.

I nodded.

"Eric," she said carefully, "changed it. Without consulting anyone. Eric began to suspect that his wife was not so responsible as one could wish. Eric began to suspect that his wife, in his absence, would fall prey to the first con man who came along. Eric, dear, dear Eric, decided that Mardee had carried the baby for this long, she might as well carry the baby a while further. He set it up—and I did not find this out until this morning—so that *I* have charge of his estate. All the bills come to me and I get to pay them. Clara gets no more than walking-around money without my specific approval."

"How much is walking-around money?" I asked cautiously.

This time Mardee's laughter was bitter. "Only a thousand dollars a week, isn't it pitiful? How is the poor woman going to survive on it? Of course, I draw a salary for my trouble, but believe me, it doesn't begin to match Clara's...walking-around money."

"Under bond, I suppose?"

"Oh, no." Mardee stubbed out the newest cigarette in a bowl she'd apparently brought from the kitchen, there being no ashtrays around, and immediately lit another one. "He trusted me, you see. So I serve without bond. And on top of that he made me residuary legatee, there being, in his opinion, nobody else."

"What happened to Amon Carter Museum?"

Mardee shrugged. "How should I know? Perhaps he got mad at it. Perhaps it ceased to interest him. So you see..." Viciously, she stubbed out the newest cigarette without smoking it. "You see, I can't let—dear—dear—Clara kill herself on the highway. Somebody, like maybe you, might begin to wonder a little too much just exactly why I did it."

"AND THEN WHAT?" Captain Millner asked, as I was telling him later that afternoon what had happened.

"I went on asking questions, of course. I really don't think Mrs. Huffman knew Helen Thorne at all; Xanax or no Xanax, she'd remember—"

"Unless she did commit the murders and she's blotted out all memory of it. That does happen, you know."

"I know that," I said. "But... even suppose she did kill her husband, I just don't think she could have gotten away from Mardee Hamilton long enough to do the other one."

"Maybe not, at least without Mardee Hamilton knowing it," Captain Millner agreed. "But if Hamilton is as protective of her as you indicate she is, could Hamilton be covering up for her?"

I couldn't say that I didn't think she would, because I didn't know whether she would or not. But I was pretty sure she wasn't, and I said that.

"Deb, this is very unsatisfactory," Captain Millner said. "You're convinced the kid didn't do it, you're convinced Mrs. Huffman didn't do it, you're convinced Ms. Hamilton didn't do it, so who the heck do you suppose *did* do it?"

"There's some factor none of us know about," I said, "and I don't know what it is."

"Obviously not. Have you charted?"

"Not yet. Actually I have, mentally, but not on paper for anybody else to look at."

"Then do it. Now."

That was not unreasonable, and as soon as I had dictated supplementary reports on tape, for Millie to put on the computer as soon as she had time, I got out the big paper we use for charting.

I had better explain charting. When we have a series of apparently similar, but not obviously linked, crimes, it is essential to figure out what the link is, because the solution to the case is going to lie somewhere in that linkage. The chart looks for every possible point of similarity or relationship, no matter how vague and apparently insignificant, between and among the victims. Do they shop at the same grocery store? Fill prescriptions at the same pharmacy? Jog in the same park? Attend the same church? Check out books in the same branch library?

I soon found that I did not have enough information to do a chart; the mental one I had been making was woefully inadequate. I knew, because somebody had told me, that Eric Huffman had been an Episcopalian. I did not know what church, if any, Helen Thorne had attended. I didn't know where, or even whether, either victim shopped, filled prescriptions, or checked out books; I was pretty sure Eric didn't jog at all, and my guess would have been that Helen didn't.

What I did know—the *only* connection I knew— was that they had both belonged to the same computer net, and had computers that had recently been invaded by a virus.

But that connection, although it didn't rule out physical contact, made it at least unlikely. And very few murders are done without physical contact. Certainly ax murders aren't.

That sounds like a joke. Of course, letter bombs and that sort of thing are done without physical contact. But that's not what I mean. What I mean is, very few murders—with the exception of politically motivated crimes, of course, and casual crime such as murder arising out of robbery—evolve in anybody's mind without enough physical contact to also create some degree of hatred, loathing, or other mental and emotional reaction. And an ax murder in particular is a murder of—

Then I mentally stopped short.

What is it a murder of? This was the first ax murder—all right, hatchet murder, to be precise—I had ever worked. I didn't really know what might be in the mind and emotions of the killer. But I knew somebody who might know.

And it was now 4:10 P.M. and I was working on my own time, something both my husband and my superior officer have repeatedly urged me not to do. Leaving the half-completed chart, I went out into the main squad room. "I need more information to finish it," I told Captain Millner, who of course was working on his own time.

"I thought you probably would. Get to it tomorrow."

And before I went *home,* I told myself, I was going to run by the hospital, where I had not been since Thursday, four days ago.

As I GOT off the elevator on the intensive care floor, I heard a click-click-click that certainly wasn't anybody's shoes, and then I did a double take as I saw a dog—not a guide dog, not any kind of special dog at all, just an ordinary garden-variety dog, and probably a mongrel at that—on a leash, trotting purposefully, and slightly sideways, as dogs so often trot, down the hall. I meant to ask somebody what the dog was doing there, but I forgot all about the dog when I stepped into Lori's room.

Lori did not look like Sleeping Beauty. Not only is it impossible to imagine Sleeping Beauty with all those wires and tubes attached, but also her hair— which she had been growing long in deference to Hal's participation in the male insistence that long hair, because it is so attractive to the beholder (holder?), is worth the time and trouble keeping it decent involves—scarcely fitted one's mental picture of Sleeping Beauty. Except where it had been clipped and shaved to allow the surgeons easy access to her skull, it lay straight and clumped together—not quite matted, because Donna had kept it as clean and combed as she could, given the situation, but certainly not as clean and bouncy and shiny as Lori normally would have kept it.

She may have been restless a few days ago. She wasn't restless now. But neither was she drawing into that fetal position that the hopelessly brain-dead seem to move into, the position that I first saw years ago, when an assault victim did not, despite everyone's prayers, die within that year and a day after the beating that is necessary to establish the beating as the cause of death and the death as a murder. The DA had the victim brought into the courtroom, so that the jury could see exactly what had been done to her, to dispel that "Sleeping Beauty" mental picture the layman so often has of the long-term comatose patient.

Not that it did a whole lot of good. There still wasn't anything more serious than aggravated assault and aggravated battery that the man could be convicted of.

We didn't even have a suspect for the person who'd done this to Lori and kept on going.

I'd expected Donna would be gone, as her four to twelve shift actually begins with muster at three-thirty. But she was still there. I asked, and she said, "Sergeant said to take my time getting in. I've been doing that some lately."

I nodded. "Any change?" I asked softly, as if somehow, in my subconscious mind, I thought Lori was asleep and we should speak quietly so as not to wake her up—though in my conscious mind, if I had thought speaking would wake her up, I would have stood right there and shouted.

Donna shook her head. "No," she said, softly too. "Nothing at all. She just lies there. It's just . . . Deb, I'm beginning to wonder if she's going to just lie there forever . . . and ever . . . and ever . . . and what will I do if she does?"

I didn't know how to answer that. I took a couple of steps closer and touched, not Donna's hand, but Lori's hand. It was warm, and her fingers curled around mine. I would have liked to think that was volitional, but I didn't. It is an instinct, one that babies are born with and one that vanishes within a few weeks after birth, as the conscious mind takes over more and more and drives instinct deeper underground. If that instinct were surfacing again now . . .

I didn't want to think of what that might mean.

And I had to leave, to go home to my own family, even if I did feel like a rat for doing it.

But I had no right to feel that way. The fact was that although Donna didn't have a lot of friends, Lori, who went to church as well as school with Hal, did. There could have been any number of people, any number of concerned adults, up here to sit with Lori. But Donna didn't want them. She'd accepted me, grudgingly, because she'd already accepted me as a potential mother-in-law of her daughter, but she wouldn't accept anybody else. I couldn't do anything about that.

That knowledge didn't stop me from feeling like a rat all the way home.

I quit feeling like a rat, and began feeling like a very harassed woman, about two seconds after I walked in the door.

Shane was the only one home; Harry presumably was still at the library, which meant Cameron was still with May Rector. I didn't know where Hal was. He couldn't possibly have headed for the hospital—Harry was still gone in the pickup truck. (Well, actually, he could, if he'd managed to mooch a ride from somebody, and he had plenty of sympathetic friends. If he didn't show up in the next few minutes I'd check on that.)

I could have worried about Harry, but in view of the fact that his computer was visibly intact I decided not to...and if you believe that, I've got some ocean-front property in Arkansas I'd like to sell you. I was worried out of my mind. But Harry is constitutionally incapable of being on time for anything, and always has been.

I wouldn't worry right now, I told myself. I'd wait and worry later. Right now I'd do something useful. If I could think of something useful. And with my family, I generally don't have too much trouble thinking of something useful to do.

The house was preternaturally clean, which meant Shane should have been proud of himself. The fact that he was walking around sideways as if he hoped to disappear without actually leaving suggested to me that he had done something that he knew I wasn't going to be happy about when I found out about it. His words confirmed my suspicions.

"Hey, Deb," he said, in that offhand way males have when they are aware they must have done something stupid, are not quite sure what it is, and are very sure they don't want to discuss it, "which way does the washing machine dial turn?"

"Clockwise," I said, suddenly feeling slightly sick at my stomach.

"That's what I was afraid of."

I headed for the garage, to check on what damage he had done to the washing machine. Laundry was piled everywhere, he'd apparently stripped all the beds (I wondered, had he also remade them?), gathered up all the laundry from all over the house, and then made no effort whatever to sort by color or fabric. The load in the machine, which included white sheets, black socks, denim jeans, and khaki pants, was at least twice as large as it should have been. But fortunately it developed that he hadn't turned the dial so far backward that the machine was nonfunctional; it was merely that it now started, for the main cycle, on what appeared to be the middle of the last spin for the delicate cycle, which as it happens I never use anyway.

So all I had to do was get the wad of sheets, et cetera, out of the washer (trailing soap powder all the while), sort the laundry, pour some soap powder in and get the machine started so that the soap powder and the water would mix on the ''low'' water level, thrust a load of laundry into the machine, and turn the machine onto the ''high'' water level so that it would go on filling now that the detergent was already dissolved in the water.

No, I don't use bleach. I also don't use hot water, unless somebody has the crud and I want to kill germs. I would like to say all this is out of respect for the environment, but actually it's because I can't afford that much hot water. Besides that, the clothes get just about as clean and they last about four times longer if they're not constantly badgered by bleach and hot water.

''I, uh, started dinner,'' Shane offered, when I finally reentered the house through the kitchen door, that being the only door out of the garage unless you open the door the car uses when we put the car in the garage, which is approximately never.

''Fine,'' I said mechanically, and then stopped short, at the sight of an empty box of Uncle Ben's Whole Grain Brown Rice, Fast Cooking, Ready in 10 Minutes. ''Shane,'' I said, ''that was a brand new box.''

Shane looked puzzled. ''Yeah,'' he agreed.

''So where's the rest of it?''

''I cooked it.'' He gestured toward my largest covered saucepan, which was sitting closed on the stove.

"Shane," I said, "that box contains fifteen servings of rice. Counting Cameron, who does not yet eat very much from the table, and Hal, who does not like rice, and you and me and Harry, there will be five people for dinner tonight. What were you planning besides rice?"

"Well, there's this box of fish sticks . . ."

There were forty-eight fish sticks. He had cooked them all. Already. It takes twenty minutes to cook fish sticks, and I normally don't start them until everybody is already sitting down.

He had chopped up an entire head of cabbage to make cole slaw. I am the only one in the family who willingly eats cole slaw, and anyway the slaw should have been started hours ago if it was to be edible at suppertime.

We had eaten fish sticks and cole slaw three days ago.

"Shane," I said, "I'll make the dinners from now on, okay?"

"Is there something wrong?"

"You've cooked enough for about ten people at the very least, just for starters."

"Oh." He looked sadly at his preparations. "Well, I had this job one time cooking for an offshore drilling rig."

"How many people were on the drilling rig?"

"Twenty. So I don't know how to cook for less than twenty people."

If he routinely cooked the fish sticks before starting the cole slaw, he also didn't know how to cook
for twenty people, I thought but did not say. "How
long did you keep the job?"

"Oh, until the next supply boat came and then
they sent me back ashore on it. It's the darnedest
thing, Deb, I don't know why it is, but I just can't
seem to keep a job. And I'm a real good worker."

Right, I thought, as I dragged sheets out of the
linen closet and began to remake my bed. You're a
real good worker, and I wish you would go and
work about five thousand miles away from me.

But of course, if he tried to leave I'd have to stop
him. So I just finished remaking my bed, and then
I went and got Cameron and brought him home after the inevitable small talk with May Rector, and I
tried to think of something I could do with the
chopped-up cabbage, since it was far too late to use
it for slaw.

Peppered cooked cabbage, and if anybody didn't
like it that was tough.

Maybe I'd go to bed early tonight. Or on the other
hand maybe I wouldn't because I had to talk with
Susan Braun either tonight on my own time or tomorrow during her work time, which she tended not
to like at all.

Nuts, I thought ungratefully, and decided I'd
better call her now rather than wait until after supper, when she might be even busier.

EIGHT

"WHY DON'T YOU have dinner with me?" Susan proposed.

I hesitated. It was tempting. It was *very* tempting, particularly since I was sure Harry would be home soon, so I wouldn't have to worry about Cameron. Harry had lately developed an inexplicable and previously unknown reluctance to miss the television news for just about any reason, except of course his Thursday night class. Well, I say lately; actually he developed the attachment to the news during the Persian Gulf War and has kept it ever since. I was tired of Harry, tired of Hal, extremely tired of Shane—in fact, at the moment I was even tired of myself. I was tired of everybody with the possible exception of Cameron and Rags, and I was even tired of them when Cameron whined or decorated the wall with the contents of his diaper, or when Rags scratched me or helped herself to my breakfast cereal before I was through with it and ready to give the remaining milk in the bowl to her. "Where and what time?" I asked.

"Cattleman's. Six-thirty." Susan is well aware of the difficulty I have in getting away early, but on the other hand she also knows that if I wait too long to eat I get very, very grouchy and even, at times, a little disoriented—certainly too disoriented to drive across town by myself.

"I'll be there."

Feeling slightly more cheerful at the thought of a supper that did *not* consist of forty-eight stale fish sticks and fifteen servings of cold brown rice, I transferred the first load of laundry to the dryer (Shane having now parked himself in front of the television set with the obvious feeling of a job well done), put the cabbage on to simmer, and spooned a little of the rice into a bowl, added a little mushroom soup and a little tuna fish, got out a few dabs of peas and carrots and put them in another bowl, heated the mess in the microwave until it was only slightly warm, and placed Cameron in his high chair.

He is now at the age when he wants to feed himself; actually, he's been at that age for quite a while, but he's getting much more proficient at it. This is, of course, a horrendous sight for all mothers, but if a baby is not allowed to feed himself when he decides he wants to, he is likely to balk horribly when his mother, several months or years later, decides *she* wants her pride and joy to feed himself.

Sometimes Cameron arrives back from May's house extremely unhungry, so I didn't know what to expect of him this time. Fortunately he decided he was hungry, and furthermore tuna casserole (which we usually refer to as Something Different, because the first time I made it, it was) and peas and carrots were *exactly* what he wanted. This meant that somewhat less than usual of the casserole and the peas and carrots landed on the floor or in his hair. He finished off with vanilla ice cream—so deep was Hal's misery that he hadn't even eaten all the ice cream in at least a week, and I was going to have to get some more because we were running out of it normally, which in this household has been un-heard of for at least the last six years.

I hoped I wasn't going to have to get Hal into treatment for depression on top of everything else. If Lori recovered, probably Hal would too, but if Lori didn't…if Lori didn't, I didn't even want to try to figure out what I was going to do about Hal.

Five-fifteen. Surely Harry would be arriving home any minute. I didn't want to have the ensuing argument in front of Shane, but how was I going to get rid of Shane? That was simple enough; I handed him three dollars out of my purse and told him to walk down to Stop 'n Go and get a half gallon of ice cream, and he could play video games with the change.

Ice cream costs under two dollars. Depending on how good at the video games he was, that ought to keep him busy anywhere from fifteen to forty-five or so minutes, in addition to the twelve minutes' walk each way.

Harry came bounding in about ten minutes after Shane left, while I was still bathing Cameron in the kitchen sink (no, I wash the dishes in the dishwasher, of course). "Why," I demanded, "did you go off and leave Cameron with Shane?"

Harry came through the living room into the (alleged) dining room to stare into the (alleged) kitchen at me. "Because I had research to do, or have you forgotten my—"

"I have not forgotten your MBA course," I retorted, "but you appear to have forgotten just exactly why Shane is staying here."

"He's staying here because he's a witness in a murder," Harry said, "and you don't want him taking off."

"He's staying here because he's a *material* witness, for which read *suspect,* in a murder," I said, "and I don't exactly want him locked up."

"Yeah, but you don't really think he did it."

"That doesn't mean I want to gamble my baby's life—"

"Deb, if you really think he's a murderer, then you're gambling the whole family's lives, and you ought to lock him up yourself."

"Quit being reasonable at me!" I screamed, very unreasonably. "I don't really think he's a murderer and you know I don't!"

"I don't see how you could think that," Harry commented. "It's thirteen miles from here to Helen's Club and Shane hasn't got wheels. Even Shane's not stupid enough to walk all over Fort Worth carrying a bloody ax."

"A hatchet."

"What?"

"The murders were done with a hatchet. One that came from the Huffmans' house. I found it behind the restaurant. Sort of behind."

"Then where, pray tell, was Shane supposed to have stashed this hatchet between murders? On the floor of Cameron's bedroom, with the rest of his stuff?"

"Oh, stop it!" I yelled. "You know I don't really think he did it!"

"Then why do you care if I leave him to babysit Cameron?"

"Because he's totally irresponsible and you know it as well as I do," I said. "What do you think he'd do if Cameron got hold of a bottle of detergent or Lysol and tried to drink it? Or even got hold of your shotgun and—"

"I don't keep loaded shotguns around the house," Harry said. "I do have a little bit of sense."

"Harry, damn it..." I wailed, and Cameron, having apparently listened to all the quarreling he wanted to and then some, began to wail even louder. *"Now* look what you've done!"

"What I've done?" Harry came on into the kitchen, which was a tight squeeze—this is a one-person kitchen at best, and I've frequently wondered if it was meant even to be that much—and picked up the towel, then picked up Cameron in the towel. "Why don't you take a nap?"

"I'm meeting Susan at Cattleman's at six-thirty and I haven't made supper for you guys yet." That reminded me to turn off the heat under the cabbage, so I did.

"It looks pretty made to me," Harry replied, glancing over the stove and grimacing at the cabbage, "and you know if you're supposed to meet Susan at six-thirty she won't be there until six-forty-five at the earliest. You've got time to lie down until six-fifteen."

"Six," I said. "I have to comb my hair and so forth after I get up."

"Susan won't care whether you comb your hair."

"I will."

"Okay, six," Harry agreed. "But it's not even five-thirty yet. Go lie down."

"But don't leave Cameron with Shane anymore," I said.

"I won't. I shouldn't have this time, but I'm so far behind on this course I wasn't even thinking. I'm afraid I'm going to have to drop it and take it over, and that'll put me way behind."

That was perfectly true. His courses come in an exactly prescribed sequence, with all the students that entered at the same time considered one "class" and taking the same courses in the same order, so that if he dropped this course he'd wind up in a different class, having to start over making the friendships that were vitally important, since the curriculum is based at least half on committee and group work.

Harry, too, had been worrying about Lori.

I went to lie down for an hour, after placing Harry, who was now heroically diapering and dressing Cameron, on his honor to remember to wake me up at six. It wasn't that I was afraid he'd forget; I was just afraid he'd get so sorry for me because I was so tired that he'd decide to let me sleep.

But this time he didn't; he woke me at six just as he had promised, and I was almost but not quite pleased enough with that to forget about his taking off earlier without thinking about Cameron's safety. I felt a little guilty, a few minutes later, about leaving Harry and Hal, who had arrived at home while I was asleep, to eat forty-eight fish sticks, fifteen servings of rice, and a large quantity of boiled cabbage for supper while I went off to dine on steak and baked potatoes. But I didn't feel guilty enough not to do it.

"YOU'RE SURE IT wasn't the wife," Susan said.

I nodded. "Well, as sure as I get. You know what I mean."

"And you're sure it wasn't the secretary."

I nodded again.

"Then chances are there's another woman involved that you haven't located yet." I must have looked puzzled, because Susan went on, "Deb, surely you know that an ax murder is more often than not a woman's crime.''

In one part of my mind I might have known that, but it wasn't in the forefront, the thinking portion, of my mind.

''Axes and poison,'' Susan said precisely, folding her napkin and signaling the waiter. ''I'll have the cheesecake, please, with strawberry topping. Deb?''

''Nothing else for me.''

Her attention back on me, Susan said, ''Of course, the majority of murders, numerically speaking, are done by men. I don't know whether that's genetic or cultural, and I don't think anybody else knows either, for all the gallons of ink that have been spilt arguing about it. But poison or axes, they're both statistically more likely to be done by women. If a man does use one of them, he's...well, he feels weak.''

''So why do you think that is?'' I asked, momentarily interested more in the larger problem than in my own case.

Susan shrugged. ''The Freudians would say one thing, the behaviorists another. The Freudians...'' She made a face. If she belonged to any school of psychiatric thought at all, which I often doubted, she leaned more toward a syncretism of Jungianism and behaviorism. ''The Freudians, I suspect, would say that the poison is an extension and perversion of the female nurturing and the ax murder is an extension and perversion of cutting the umbilical cord.

But then the Freudians have a distorted view of sex
and gender, particularly of female sex and gender.
Everything is the quest for the phallus, which isn't
necessarily the penis, and even cutting the umbilical cord becomes a symbolic castration, so of course
the ax murder is also a symbolic castration gone to
extremes.''

"So how does poison fit into the quest for the
phallus?'' I'd heard Susan on this topic before.

"Oh, I don't know," she said dismissingly. "All
that stuff is gibberish to me. You know Freud decided women who reported childhood incest were
making it up. So much for Freud and the Freudians. Anyhow, on to the behaviorists. I don't really
know, but just guessing, it's easier for a woman to
use poison because she's usually the one preparing
the food, and as for the ax . . . well, I do have some
strong opinions about that.''

"Which are?'' Susan's strong opinions, though
not necessarily always right, tend to be more or less
interesting.

"It's just, anybody coming from a position of
weakness . . . It's overkill. Not just the ax, even a
gun. If you feel you're coming from a position of
strength, you only have to kill the person once.
When you . . . I don't like to bring up bad memories, but when you killed that man, how many times
did you pull the trigger?''

"Once," I said, wishing the memory would, over the years, become a little less intense. "It was all I needed to."

"All right, but if you had felt yourself weak—impotent, not in the sexual sense but in the overall sense of power, and that, by the way, seems to be at least as much as anything what the Freudians mean by the phallus, overall power, empowerment, let's say rather, than power per se... Where was I?" She brushed hair back from her eyes. She'd recently given up on braids and gotten a cut and curly perm, but it wasn't staying put any better than the braids had done.

"Talking about ax murders and impotence."

"All right, if you felt yourself powerless—disempowered, let's say—you'd be afraid pulling the trigger once wasn't enough. You'd pull it until the gun was empty and then keep on pulling it. Haven't you noticed that an ax murder is always overkill?"

"Since this is the first one, or rather the first two, that I ever worked," I replied, "I can't say that I've had the opportunity to notice that."

"Well, but reading the literature on the subject—"

"I don't," I said flatly.

"Deb, you really should read more."

"When would I have time?" That was a cop-out—I read plenty of fiction—but Susan didn't spot it.

"*I* find time, and I have a hospital to run."

"You don't have a teenager and a baby. By the way, when are you getting married?"

"Don't rush me."

"I'm not. But your fiancé—"

"Will wait," she said complacently. "You keep distracting my attention. Where was I this time?"

"Getting married," I said a bit flippantly, and she glared at me and then laughed.

"Maybe I see getting married as disempowerment. I think I need to discuss that with Brad."

"How do two psychiatrists get married?" I asked, and answered my own question. "The same way porcupines make love—very, very carefully. That cheesecake looks good. I think I do want some after all."

The waiter, looking vaguely displeased at my indecision, departed in the direction of the kitchen.

"I think I'm still trying to talk about ax murders," Susan said. "They're always overkill. Remember Lizzie Borden?"

"She was acquitted."

"Rrri-i-ght," Susan said. "And ostracized for the rest of her life, by people who refused to convict her legally because she was 'one of us' but who sentenced her in their own way. Anyway, I'm talking about the ditty, not the actual case. Remember it?"

"Lizzie Borden took an ax, gave her mother forty whacks. When she saw what she had done, gave her father forty-one," I recited, singsongy. "Anyway, it was her stepmother, not her mother. And the numbers, if anything, were underestimates rather than overestimates.''

"I thought you didn't read case histories."

"I read that one."

"Then you see what I mean. Overkill. And remember that case in McKinney or wherever it was a few years back? Nice, churchgoing woman chopped her neighbor to mincemeat and then went to a children's birthday party, taking her children *and* her victim's children.''

As I'd been thinking about that case myself lately, I just nodded and began to eat the cheesecake, which had somehow appeared on the table in the midst of that discussion. "But what does that have to do with empowerment?"

"If you're strong, or feel strong," Susan said, "you only have to kill someone once. You're pretty sure the person will stay dead. But if you're weak, or feel weak—that is, if you are or feel disempowered, whether because you're of a gender that's discriminated against or a race or religion that's discriminated against, or just because you personally feel disempowered, you're not altogether sure that if you kill somebody that person will stay dead. So you kill, and kill, and kill. You pull the trigger till you're out of bullets and then keep on pulling it just in case there might be another bullet somewhere that you missed the first trip around the cylinder. Like that case in Los Angeles last year—the high-speed chase and then the cops beat up the driver and somebody videotaped it. What happened was, the high-speed chase scared the piss out of the cops, thus disempowering them, thus enraging them, so the guy who created the situation, thus causing the disempowerment, got the shit beat out of him."

"Which doesn't excuse the cops," I pointed out, ignoring her scatological mixed metaphors. "Police are supposed to have more self-control than that."

"That's perfectly true," Susan said. "But you see what I mean. It happens all the time, in war, for example, on the personal scale or the global scale. Saddam Hussein burned the Kuwaiti oil fields because he felt disempowered by the Allied victory. The Ku Klux Klan resulted from the Confederate disempowerment. *Do* you see what I mean?"

"Yes, but that doesn't mean I have to like it."

"Oh, of course you don't like it," Susan agreed readily. "I don't like it either. But that's at least partly because we—you and I—don't feel overwhelmingly disempowered. But back to ax murders. If you're disempowered, and therefore enraged, you grab an ax and hack, and hack, and hack, and never mind that the victim's already dead, because the victim might *not* be really dead, or not dead enough. I don't think I've ever heard of an ax murderer that used just one blow, the fatal one, and then stopped. Have you? Lizzie Borden certainly didn't, and that woman in McKinney or wherever it was..."

I shivered, or maybe shuddered. "With those two, I didn't think of disempowerment. It looked like anger to me."

"Oh, there's always an element of rage mixed in with disempowerment. I've mentioned that already. The slave always hates the master, whether it's a real master-slave relationship or just a perceived one. So yes, the rage is certainly there, but there's still the feeling of coming from a position of weakness, and feeling weak causes us to feel enraged. Disempowerment is *always* accompanied by rage."

"You said that twice."

"Thing is, the disempowerment triggers the rage."

"You know what Captain Millner's going to say when I tell him this?" I asked. "He's going to say, 'Spare me the psychological gobbledygook.'"

"Then spare him the psychological gobbledygook," Susan answered lightly. "You don't have to tell him why you're looking for another woman, or looking harder at the two women you already know are in the case. Surely he at least knows that an ax murder is likely to be done by a woman."

"Oh, he probably knows that," I agreed. "If it turned out to be either of the two women I know about, it would be the wife. I don't think the secretary feels this...disempowerment you keep talking about."

"From what you've told me, I'd feel inclined to agree," Susan said.

"And I still don't have any connection between Eric Huffman and Helen Thorne."

"Don't you?" Susan said. "Think about it some more. I think you do."

"Susan, if you've figured something out and you're not telling me—"

"Clara Huffman didn't know who Helen Thorne was . . . or said she didn't. And you think she's telling the truth. Mardee Hamilton did know who Helen Thorne was."

"But—"

"Don't interrupt, and don't chase wild hares. Helen Thorne didn't have anything to do with Mardee Hamilton's sexual inclinations, because if that had been the connection there would have been no reason at all for Eric Huffman to be killed."

"Unless Helen was having some sort of an affair with Mardee and broke it off to have some sort of an affair with Eric," I pointed out.

Susan stared at me in momentary astonishment. "Sometimes your mind is twistier than mine is. In that case, Helen would have been killed first, of course."

"Why 'of course'?"

"Take my word for it. Anyway, we've already agreed that Mardee Hamilton wouldn't use an ax."

"She might if jealousy were involved."

"Deb, you're chasing wild hares. Now quit it."

"I don't see why that is any wilder a hare than any other hare."

"Fine, chase it all you want to," Susan said, "but you're not going to get anywhere with it."

"I'm not getting anywhere with anything," I retorted, "and the only connection I know I have is that damned computer network."

"In your opinion," Susan said carefully, "bearing in mind that unlike most people who say they're good judges of character, you really are a good judge of character—in your opinion, is Mardee Hamilton likely to be a murderer? Never mind whether she'd kill; anybody will kill, given the right situation, no matter how convinced they are that they wouldn't. But is she likely to be a murderer?"

"No, I don't think so. But if she was she'd think it out very, very carefully."

"What about Clara Huffman?"

"She would be, but I don't think she could be."

"So you're claiming extreme disempowerment for her."

"If you want to put it that way."

"So she's mentally and emotionally capable of being an ax murderer, if she's that disempowered. But you don't think she'd be able to?"

"I don't know. She might. But I don't think she'd have been able to get away from Mardee long enough to kill Helen Thorne, and I don't know why she'd have wanted to anyway."

"Oh, come on," Susan said, "you've already postulated an affair between Eric Huffman and Helen Thorne."

"But that was when I was chasing wild hares."

"Maybe not all of them were wild."

"Susan," I said carefully, "I have no, repeat no, reason to assume that Eric Huffman and Helen Thorne were in any way emotionally involved."

"But I'll lay you any odds you want to name that you're going to find out that they were. And Mardee knew about it. The secretary always knows, whether the wife does or not."

"Then are you saying you think Clara Huffman *did*—"

"Possibly. Or possibly not. Who else, either female or otherwise, feeling disempowered, would have had a reason?"

"Nobody that I know of. What do you think?"

Susan shrugged. "Now, *that* I do not know."

"I want to be sure I understand what we've been saying," I said carefully. "We—or maybe you—are saying that Eric Huffman and Helen Thorne were having an affair, and Mardee Hamilton knew about it but maybe Clara Huffman didn't, and either Clara Huffman or somebody else who was feeling...disempowered—I'm still not comfortable with that word—killed them because of it."

"Oh, I didn't say that at all," Susan said.

"It certainly sounded to me as if you did. Then what did you say?"

"Well, I do think that you're going to find that Eric and Helen were involved, because there's no other possible connection; this computer link may be how they met, but it's not a likely reason for murder. And I do think Mardee Hamilton knew about it, and I do think whoever murdered Eric and Helen was somebody who was coming from a real or perceived state of disempowerment, but I don't necessarily think it's because they were having an affair."

"Sometimes you make my stomach hurt," I said. "Or maybe my head."

Susan shrugged. "Sorry. How is our namesake doing?"

"Just fine, last time I saw her. Except for being overloaded with names."

"How true, how true," Susan said. "But it was sweet of them all the same."

"I think it was more Olead than Becky." My daughter—second daughter, that is—and son-in-law, when their baby daughter arrived last month, named the unfortunate child Susan Debra, in honor of Susan and me, as they consider the two of us jointly responsible for the fact that Olead is both sane and free. They're calling her Debra, because Susan is still using her name and I'm only using part of mine. Remembering how much I hated being Debra, I am sorry for her, particularly since it will be harder for her to whack it down to Deb as I did because that's the part of the name that I'm using.

I've decided to call her Dee, if Becky and Olead will let me get away with it.

That, of course, remains to be seen.

This was their second child in exactly twelve and a half months; the first was a boy they were calling Jim in memory of Olead's father. They could, of course, afford two babies in two years, economically at least, though I wondered how anybody could manage two in diapers easily. Becky had assured me it couldn't be *much* worse than having twins.

But that was neither here nor there, at the moment. "In view of the fact that we both have to work tomorrow..." I began.

"I guess we'd better go home," Susan finished, and grabbed the check from under my fingers. "I've got it."

"It's my turn," I protested.

"You get it next time. *After* you've cleared the case. If I was right you get to bring me here again. If I was wrong you get to take me to...uh... McDonald's."

"You got it," I said.

WHEN I GOT HOME, shortly after ten o'clock, Pat greeted me in the driveway, as usual wagging from the shoulders back to make up for his near-total lack of tail. "Whuff," he said amiably, and then, realizing I was not Lori, he sat down abruptly. I don't know who he thought I was to start with, as Lori never—well, hardly ever—arrived here after ten o'clock at night.

I opened the gate and stopped short. Shane was up in the mesquite tree—a feat in itself, considering how thorny mesquite trees are—and was wielding a machete with great vigor. "I thought I'd cut off some of these low branches," he said cheerfully. "That way nobody'll bump their heads on them anymore, and besides that we can dry the branches and use them for mesquite barbecuing this summer. Won't that be nice?"

What's this *we*, I thought; I certainly didn't plan on still having Shane with us in the summer. But I didn't say that right now because I had other things to say. "Shane, it's the middle of the night," I pointed out.

"Oh, it's not that late. And the moon is nice and bright."

"The moon is nice and bright and the temperature is forty-two degrees. Where'd you get the machete?"

"It was in the truck. I like things like that, don't you?"

"No, Shane," I said, "frankly, I do *not* like things like that. Now drop the machete on the ground, climb carefully out of the tree so you don't impale yourself on the way down, put the machete back in the truck, and take yourself in the house."

"But I was just—"

"I don't want to hear it." I grabbed Pat's collar, so he'd be out of the way while the machete dropped to the ground. Then I took Pat inside.

I know what Harry says about disciplining the dog. But maybe keeping a pit bull inside wouldn't be such a bad idea after all.

The cats' bowls were inside, not outside on the hood of the truck, and they were full not of cat food but of fish sticks. There were three open pizza boxes on the table. It was not too hard to deduce that (a) the fish sticks, having been cooked two hours too soon, had been too stale to eat; (b) Harry had sent out for pizza, Hal having by that time presumably left for the hospital in the truck; and (c) the fish sticks had proven to be too stale for even the cats to eat.

Pat whuffed at the fish sticks hopefully. Even he turned away from them. He looked at me imploringly and whuffed again. "Sorry, dog," I said, "you've had your supper, and the baby's asleep. You can't go wake him up to kiss him."

"Deb," Harry asked, "why did you bring the dog inside?"

"I thought it would be nice to have the dog inside," I answered airily.

Harry had too much sense to question that statement, so I went off toward the bedroom, followed by the dog. His claws tap-tapped on the floor just the way the dog's claws in the hospital had sounded.

And by the way, what *was* that dog doing on the intensive care floor of the hospital?

NINE

SOMETIME IN THE middle of the night—what my mother used to call the wee, small hours of the morning—I awakened to the crunching of Pat deciding the fish sticks were still edible after all. A little while after that I was reminded of one of the reasons why Harry and I had long since ruled out indoor dogs. Pat politely informed us that he had to go outside. He had to go outside *now,* he added, when neither of us showed any inclination to get up to attend to doors.

"If you're going to keep that damned dog inside," Harry said, "we've got to get a dog door."

"We don't have a dog door now."

"You let him in; you let him out."

"*I* have to get up to go to work in the morning."

There was a long silence, during which Pat whined again, slightly more urgently. Finally Harry said, "Oh, hell." He sat up, turned on the bedside lamp, started to stand up, and knocked the lamp over. It landed bulb side down on the bed. "Oh, hell," he said again, and picked the lamp up and sat it back on the table. He finished getting up, escorted Pat to the patio door, let the dog out, and headed back into the bedroom.

By this time I was sitting up and sniffing. "Uh, Harry," I said, "is something burning?"

"Not that I know of." He sat down on the edge of the bed.

"I wouldn't lie down if I were you."

"How come?"

"Because I think your side of the bed is on fire."

He looked at the blackened, smoking circle near the corner of the bed where the light bulb had touched. "I don't think it's on fire," he said. "I think it's just sort of singed."

"Don't lie down anyway." I got up, went to the kitchen, filled a quart measuring cup with water, brought it back to the bedroom, and poured it on the blackened spot. There was a distinct sizzling sound. "That ought to be okay now. While I'm up, I guess I'll—"

"Yeah," Harry said, "you always do." He continued to sit on the edge of the bed while I went to, and returned from, the bathroom. "Hey, Deb, that fire's still not out."

I checked. It wasn't. There was still smoke rising, and the smoke had a distinctly acrid smell.

I took the measuring cup into the bathroom, refilled it, and dumped more water. And more. And more. Harry scratched his head. "I think we're going to have to call the fire department," he said.

"It's six miles to the fire station," I pointed out. "Do you expect the fire to just sit here and wait?"

"I guess we could haul the mattress out on the front porch."

I do not want to discuss the rest of the evening. Manhandling a large, wet, smoldering mattress out the front door, while being assisted by two excited teenagers (well, Shane wasn't exactly a teenager, but he might as well have been), two excited cats who don't like each other, and one excited pit bull, and then waiting around for the fire department to arrive with red light and siren even though they were asked to use neither, there being no immediate danger to house or property, and then trying to convince hysterical and/or nosy neighbors that, yes, everything is really all right—none of these things are altogether amusing. Of course, I had to send Hal and Shane to take—or rather, to drag—the dog inside, fire fighters being included in the list of people in uniform that Pat does not like. The fire fighters dumped what seemed like about two hundred gallons of water onto the mattress and assured us that a mattress fire is really very dangerous, because it can smolder for hours and then blaze up.

When we finally got back to bed, about four A.M., I was on the extra bed in Cameron's room (the one Shane had been using), Harry was on the couch, and both Hal and Shane were in Hal's room chattering.

But no amount of excitement in the night could—this week at least—stop Hal from getting up in time for his early morning religion class, which meant he went banging out the door and taking off in the pickup truck about five-fifteen. I was really not ready for the alarm to go off at six-thirty, and by the time Hal came back in at seven yelling, "What's for breakfast?" I felt as if I had been hit over the head with a club.

At least he was not telling me all about everything he was studying and his opinions thereof, as he did last year while he was on the prophets and other gory parts of the Old Testament. This year they were on the New Testament and had gotten to the epistles, which he found too boring to discuss at great length and in any detail.

"I'm having cereal," I said, "and you have your choice. Cereal, peanut butter, leftover pizza, or anything you want to cook yourself. And I hope," I added to Harry, "that you're going to get rid of that mattress today."

"I'll get rid of the mattress today."

"Because I don't think the trash truck will pick it up, and it's not quite what I consider an aesthetically pleasing yard ornament."

"I said I'll get rid of it."

That was true. He had said he would get rid of it. It wasn't his fault I felt like a zombie. It wasn't even his fault he got to stay home while I had to go out and face the world. That knowledge did not improve my disposition in the slightest degree. Neither did the fact that the cat—the new cat, that is; the old cat has better sense, if not better manners— had helped herself to my cereal while I was pondering these matters, so that I had to give her that bowl and get myself a new bowl.

All right, doubtless the cat would be better disciplined if I did *not* give her the old bowl of cereal while I got the new bowl, but there are times I do not have the energy to do what I know I ought to do.

Okay, what did I have to do today, I asked myself as I got the Cheerios back out.

I had to make an effort to check out Susan's belief that there was a romantic involvement between the two victims. Like Susan, I couldn't exactly figure out any reason why they would have been murdered, the way they were murdered, if there weren't some connection between them, but unlike Susan, I had to prove my conjectures at least to my own satisfaction if not to anybody else's.

"Deb, I think I'll go job hunting today. Is that okay with you?" Shane chirped. People who are that cheerful in the morning are disgusting.

"By all means, go job hunting," I said.

"Then can you drop me downtown?"

"Yeah, I'll drop you downtown." Anticipating the next question, I handed over three dollars, to cover a hamburger and bus fare home. I wished I thought he would really find a job, particularly one he was likely to keep for more than six hours, but at this time of the morning my optimism circuit doesn't work. One thing about it, though, I thought, and that is, when he's downtown he's not anywhere near my husband and my children and my home.

But that was an unworthy thought. I am supposed to be protecting all the citizenry, not just those related or otherwise connected to me.

Tuesday morning, and all was not well. Pat asked to go to work with me. I declined to allow him to.

What did I have to do today?

Find somebody who was close to Helen to talk with. Talk with Clara and Mardee again. Tell Millner why I am sniffing around Clara and Mardee again when I had already ruled them out.

It might also be a good idea to find out what, if anything, Dutch had been doing; although the case had wound up being mine, he'd caught the initial call with me and had talked with neighbors. Undoubtedly he had at least made a report.

I had, of course, to start out with Millner, who did have a certain right to be kept informed of what I was doing and why I was doing it. I decided to spare him as much of the psychological mumbo jumbo as possible, so I merely told him that Susan had reminded me that an ax murderer is often a woman. "I knew that," he said irritatingly.

"Then why didn't you remind me?"

"I didn't know you wouldn't think of it. Did your friend make any other suggestions?" He doesn't like psychology, but all the same he's aware that Susan's suggestions in the past have proven useful.

"Nothing you'd want to hear."

"Okay, so you're getting on with the charting today."

"I guess." I'd have to organize the information I got somehow, and charting was as good a way as any.

I went to my desk and started to make a list of questions I needed to ask people, but then I decided I'd better have a look at Dutch's report instead. I had suddenly—and very belatedly, but that was okay because Dutch was the one who was supposed to have been dealing with this—remembered that Clara had reported that her husband's car wasn't there when she got home.

Dutch's report didn't say that, I found when I called it up on the computer. All it said was that the victim's car, which was normally parked out front, was instead inside the garage, and complainant therefore did not see it at first and assumed it was gone.

Good. I didn't have to worry that I had neglected for over three days to put a stolen car on NCIC.

That was about all that Dutch's report said that seemed to be of any use, I thought gloomily as I read on. None of the neighbors he'd talked with had heard or seen anything; they all agreed—those few who said anything at all, that is—that Eric Huffman had left early in the morning to play golf (they were sure of that because he'd been carrying his golf bag when he'd gotten into a friend's car); his wife had left later in the morning (none of them knew where, but we did; she'd gone to get her hair done); Eric had returned later, slamming a car door and noisily telling his friend good-bye and thanks for the ride; then—wait a minute. Wait a minute.

According to one neighbor, on his return home Eric Huffman had called the police. The neighbor didn't know the purpose of the call, but a police car had arrived about thirty minutes after Eric's return home and had parked in front of the house for about twenty or thirty minutes before leaving.

It was odd that nobody had remembered that, in dispatch, when they got the call later about the murder—no, come to think of it, it wasn't odd at all, because it would have been day watch that got the earlier call, and evening watch that got the later one. And Clara wouldn't have been there when the initial call was made, so whatever Eric had called about, she wouldn't have known about it.

I needed, urgently, to talk to the patrol officer who'd gotten that first call. I telephoned dispatch and asked to have the record of that first call looked up.

Then I went on reading Dutch's report.

Somebody from dispatch called me back about fifteen minutes later, as I was making lists of questions I needed to ask. "What did you say that address was again?"

I told him.

"And the complainant's name?"

"Would have been Eric Huffman."

"Well, we can't find it. And that beat says he didn't get the call."

"Maybe whoever took the call wrote it down as *Hoffman*. And I suppose if that beat was busy somebody else could have gotten the call, if it seemed urgent."

"I'll check on that. Hold on ... No Hoffman either. And no telling who got the call, if that beat didn't."

"Keep looking," I said resignedly. "It might be out of sequence or something."

In these days of computers, reports getting out of sequence is not supposed to happen. Well, it never was *supposed* to happen, but now it's theoretically impossible. That does not, of course, make it really impossible.

They'd get back to me when they could. But locating misplaced information could take hours, and in the meantime I had other things to do.

I telephoned the Huffman residence; Mardee answered. "Could I come out this morning to ask a few more questions?" I inquired after identifying myself.

"This isn't a good time," Mardee said. "Eric's funeral is at ten, or didn't you know?"

Actually I didn't, and I should have. Often, though not always, I go to funerals—victim's funerals. The old superstition that the murderer always shows up at the funeral is just as much nonsense as is the old superstition that the murderer always returns to the scene of the crime. But *sometimes* the murderer goes to the funeral, just as *sometimes* the murderer returns to the scene of the crime. (I wondered what Susan would say about that. Would she consider those actions also signs of disempowerment, the need to be sure the victim was really dead?) And *sometimes* the police can spot something interesting in the interactions of people at the funeral.

But I was wearing slacks this morning, and I didn't want to go to a funeral in slacks.

I telephoned Helen's Club, but Leon Aristides wasn't there, nor was anybody else who knew Helen well enough to be worth my asking questions.

But somebody must have claimed the body... I called the Medical Examiner's office and got the secretary, Beverly Hart. "Just a minute," she said, "let me check." In a minute she was back. "The body was claimed by Francis Marion Thorne— that's a male name."

"I know," I said. Many unhappy men, especially in the South, have been named for the Revolutionary War hero Francis Marion. "Have you got that address and phone number?"

She gave them to me.

"Thanks, Bev."

"Good luck," she said. "This one sounds like a woolly booger."

Francis Marion Thorne lived on Pecan Street. I had to get out my Mapsco to find out where that was. Goodie, I thought a few minutes later. There were Pecan Streets in three totally different places in

Fort Worth, one in Arlington, one in Azle, one in Burleson, one in Crowley, one in Hurst, one in Keller, one in Mansfield, and one in Roanoke, to say nothing of assorted Pecan Courts, Pecan Drives, Pecan Chases, Pecan Parks, et cetera, all of which might be the right one if he'd just given his address as whatever-it-was Pecan and somebody else had added the word *Street*. I telephoned, hoping he would live in Hurst or Keller, either of which was convenient to me.

He didn't, but on the other hand he didn't live in Arlington or someplace like that, either. He also didn't live on Pecan Street; that was his business address, and for some reason—probably illegal—he had his business address rather than his home address on his driver's license, which was where the person who released the body had gotten his address. He lived in a rather nice condo just outside downtown Fort Worth. Also, and not quite incidentally, he was at home and he said I could go talk to him, though he didn't see what good it was going to do.

Neither did I. This was what is known as a fishing expedition, fishing for information, which might or might not be forthcoming.

So I drove over there, and I did not enjoy my visit.

Francis Marion Thorne was Helen's father. Lucy Thorne was Helen's mother. They were both—they insisted but did not act—far too torn up by grief to talk to me.

I started out with my carefully planned list of questions, for all the good that didn't do. The two quarreled steadily with one another even as they answered. Helen was Episcopalian, not active. They didn't know where she shopped, exercised, or went to the doctor. She'd never been married. If she had a current boyfriend they didn't know about it. She'd gone to a business school rather than college, worked for a couple of years as a secretary, decided she didn't like it. She'd then gone to work first as a hostess, then as assistant manager, then as manager for several restaurants and clubs in the area. I got names and approximate dates in case it was relevant, which it almost certainly was not.

"Could you tell me who some of her friends were?" I asked.

"Oh, you don't think she'd tell *me* who her friends were," Lucy said. "She was far too busy with her social life. You'd think she'd want me to know, but no..."

"She acted like she was ashamed of us," Marion—that was what he'd asked me to call him—said. "Never could find time for her parents, after all we gave her—"

"After all *who* gave her?" Lucy asked. "*You* couldn't find time for anybody but yourself—"

"Maybe if you'd be content with just one mink coat I could find more time for something besides working," Marion said, "but no, you had to have two—"

"One of them was a jacket, and I gave it to Helen anyway…"

I didn't see any sense in listening to much more of this, and I could certainly see why Helen had wanted to build a life of her own. Anything to get out of this atmosphere—and she'd probably had to be the "Dragon Lady" Leon Aristides described her as, in order to survive. But I pried some more, and Lucy finally disclosed, reluctantly, the name of one friend. "Monica Mulholland," she said.

"Monique," Marion corrected.

"Just because she decides to tart up her name doesn't mean I have to use it that way," Lucy said.

"It's her name," Marion said.

"*You* would defend her," Lucy retorted.

"I'm not defending her," Marion said. "I just said it's her name, and it is, isn't it?"

"Men are always like this, aren't they," Lucy said confidingly to me. "Making fools of themselves over very obvious blondes—"

"I just said it's her name," Marion repeated. "And she's a really foxy lady…tell by looking at her she's hot to trot—"

"She's very low class," Lucy assured me. "I can't see why Helen liked her."

"In what way is she lower class?"

"Oh, that bleached hair," Lucy said, patting her own champagne-blond, definitely out of a bottle, hair. "And she calls herself a chanteuse. That means she's a nightclub singer."

"In Helen's Club?" I asked, thinking that there was something to my mind a little Roaring Twentyish about a singer calling herself a chanteuse.

"Well, yes . . ."

After a little more of that I managed to escape, driving to the closest 7-Eleven to look in the telephone book for Monique Mulholland, who of course was not listed.

I called the club again; this time Leon Aristides was there. He gave me Monique's telephone number and assured me she was never awake before noon.

Tough. I was going to wake her up.

I proceeded to do just that.

"You might as well come over," she said. "I never did get back to sleep after getting the kids off to school this morning anyway."

I didn't know where to expect a chanteuse to live, but Monique Mulholland lived in a fifties-style tract house with fading green asbestos siding and a chain link fence, which enclosed a large dog of uncertain breed and the kind of yard you'd expect to find occupied by a large dog of uncertain breed and even more uncertain habits. A faded and rust-streaked green Chevrolet, fifteen years old, sat in the carport. The front yard had some unclipped hedges and a lawn that had been mowed one time less than it should have been before the cold weather came. A naked Barbie doll lay on the front walk beside an also naked GI Joe doll in a pose that suggested to me that Monique wasn't overwhelmingly careful about what her children watched on television. Either that, or the dolls had just happened to get left in that position and I had acquired a dirty mind from too many years of policing.

Monique looked to me like a natural blond, not a bleached blond; she had that fragile look that often goes with extremely fair skin. There was a pinched look about her eyes and a violet around and under them that wasn't eye shadow. She was wearing a pink nightgown, nylon, opaque, and a pink quilted housecoat. "Come in," she said. "But don't get too close to me, because I think I'm coming down with something. Either that or I'm pregnant again, and I think I'd jump off a bridge or something if I was. Just kidding. I'm sorry everything's such a mess. Four kids. Stair steps. Ten, nine, eight, seven. How many kids do you have?"

"Four," I said, "but they're a lot more widely spaced. I don't envy you." I followed her into a very cluttered, and very small, living room.

She gestured toward a chair, turned, coughed, and sat down on the couch. "How old are yours?"

I had to stop and think. "Twenty-six, twenty-two, seventeen, and almost two."

"Almost *two!* Boy! Talk about an afterthought! I'm sorry. You want to talk about Helen and I'm trying to talk about everything else but. 'Scuse me..." She ran into the bathroom.

Uncharitably, I hoped she was pregnant. That's not contagious. Most other things that lead to that kind of vomiting are.

After flushing and running water she came back, even more pale than she had been. "I might as well stop kidding myself, huh?"

"About what?"

She gestured comprehensively toward her mid-section. "I'm a month late and barfing all the time. Break out the diapers, Monica. Boy, Joe's gonna love this. Oh, well, I hated the job and now I've got a real good excuse to quit. Nobody wants to watch a pregnant chanteuse." She laughed self-derisively. "Don't you love that word? Helen insisted on it. She also said I had to be Monique, rather than Monica. Got to be French, got to be fancy. I asked her why she didn't call the club Chez Hélène or something like that and she told me not to be silly. Now I ask you, is that any sillier than Monique Mulholland, chanteuse?"

It didn't sound any sillier to me, and I said so.

"But I'll have to admit the money did come in handy," she added. "It's real good money. If I can manage to go on working three more months we can pay Joe's truck off."

"What kind of work does your husband do?"

"He drives a catering truck. You know, one of those trucks that pulls into the driveway of a work site and honks its horn about two dozen times and everybody runs up and buys goodies? Sandwiches and cookies and stuff?''

"Do you make the sandwiches and cookies and stuff?"

She laughed. "Are you kidding? The Health Department would have cats if I even looked like thinking about making that stuff here. He buys it from some kind of wholesaler. Excuse me..."

She came back a few minutes later. "The only thing that stops me barfing is Cokes, and I'm all out. I can't stop barfing long enough to dress and get in the car and go out and buy some."

My duty was clear, and I had seen a Stop 'n Go three or four blocks away. Anyway, it was obvious she wasn't going to be able to sit still long enough to answer questions until after I had gone out and bought those Cokes.

"I really wasn't surprised she got murdered," Monica said later, after swallowing half the first Coke in about fifteen seconds.

"You expected her to?"

"Oh, no, not really," Monica said. "It was just...she was living dangerously. I told her so. She was..." Monica shifted positions, sat up straighter. "She'd never been married, okay? And she's my age, we were in grade school together. Thirty-four, and you know what they say about the biological clock ticking away. Only I don't think she'd have been any good as a mother at all, she was too self-centered for that or a husband either, but *she* wanted children and to do that she wanted to be married. And besides that the club... well, she'd wanted the club a long time and she'd worked hard to get it, but it was taking so much of her time and she'd decided she wanted to be... what was it she said, a lady of leisure."

I couldn't help it. I laughed out loud, and Monica did too. "Well, that's what I told her," Monica said. "But she had the bit in her teeth. She was gonna get married, and she was gonna marry a rich man. Only problem was, all the rich men were taken."

"So what did she do?" I asked.

"She kept running after men. She kept getting boyfriends and then they didn't work out and she'd get another one and that one wouldn't work out. And then she got this one boyfriend, he was kind of old and kind of rich, I never saw him but that's what she told me, and she told me she was gonna get him one way or another. I told her that was fine, if he was available to be gotten. She told me she'd get him away from his wife. Then she could have a kid or two and by that time her boyfriend'd die and she'd have her kids and his money and then she'd really be a lady of leisure. I told her she was crazy. I told her you don't decide to 'get' somebody else's husband. Look, it was like talking to... to that wall over there. She just laughed at me and told me again she was gonna 'get' him. I told her she'd be lucky if somebody like maybe the guy's wife didn't 'get' her.

So... I'm surprised the way she was killed. But I'm not really surprised she got murdered. I figure if you can find out who her boyfriend was..." Monica looked at me interestedly. "I don't want to know. But the paper says this kind of old guy with a lot of money was murdered the same way she was. So maybe if you looked at his wife..."

I had been doing just about nothing else but, since last Friday. But of course I couldn't tell Monica that.

"Or maybe," Monica added, "he had another girlfriend and she killed Helen. Only I don't know why another girlfriend would want to kill him too. A wife, yeah, but not a girlfriend."

All that was perfectly possible, but I wasn't really sure how I was going to find it out if he did. I thanked Monica and went out to brood in the car as I drove slowly back into the main part of town.

All right, I knew he played golf. I didn't know where he played golf, but either his wife or his secretary—probably both—would certainly know that. If I could find out who he played golf with...a man might talk much more freely to his golfing companions about possible girlfriends...

Harry had told me that Eric had retired not just because of his health but also because of Clara's obsessive jealousy. Most men's identity is bound up with the work they do; if he had so little strength of identity that he found it comfortable to quit work and stay at home, then would he have a girlfriend at all?

On the other hand, maybe it wasn't a lack of strength of identity. If he had all those hobbies he apparently had, maybe his identity was bound up in the hobbies rather than the job. And maybe it was a shifting identity, like the shifting hobbies. In that case he could perfectly easily have half a dozen girl-friends.

There was something nagging at my mind and I couldn't figure out what it was. Something to do with the computer. Something Clara had told me. She'd been his accountant until he got the computer and began doing it all himself on the computer. And Clara was weak, very weak, but she wasn't stupid. The computer...

There was something about the computer that had differed in the two crime scenes and I could *not* figure out what it was.

Maybe if I looked at the crime scene pictures...

I drove in to the police station with only the periphery of my mind on driving, because the main part of my mind was concentrating on whatever it was that I couldn't seem to put a name to.

Of *what* had Clara been jealous? Not just whom, but *what?* If she was jealous of Eric's work for taking time that she felt belonged to her, what else had she been jealous of?

And was there really a connection between the two killings? Well, there had to be, but...

I parked my car, went into the police station, and went straight to ident. Irene was out, but Sarah Collins, our newest ident tech, who could undoubtedly go to work as a model if she ever got tired of policing, was there and had no trouble at all finding me the two packages of photographs.

And there it was, what had been nagging me so much. I had noticed it but not noticed it, if you know what I mean.

Eric's computer had been smashed well before Eric had been killed; there was blood splattered on the inside and back side of the computer parts. That suggested that perhaps Clara, as jealous of the computer as she had been of Eric's career, had demolished the computer, whether she remembered it now or not, before going to the beauty shop. If so, then I was going to find that whoever had answered the call to the Huffman's house had been there because of a report of vandalism. And nobody had been to the Huffman's house after the police officer until Clara got home. So if that was true, then almost certainly—I say *almost* because of course somebody could have gone there without being seen by the neighbors—it was Clara herself who murdered Eric Huffman, as difficult as I might find it to believe that.

But Helen Thorne's computer had been smashed *after* Helen's death. Computer fragments were lying on top of blood splashes, on top of fragments of flesh and blood and brain.

We had a copycat killer. And I hadn't the slightest idea how Eric Huffman's hatchet had gotten to the scene of the second crime.

Unless Mardee Hamilton—for what reason I couldn't possibly imagine—was the copycat killer.

Possibly you've noticed that I was reasoning far ahead of my data again.

TEN

I MADE IT a search warrant, not yet an arrest warrant, because I wasn't even certain I was right, much less that I would ever be able to prove it. The telephone on my desk rang while Dutch—very unenthusiastically, because he said he didn't see how we were going to find any useful evidence at all considering the circumstances—was gone to get the warrant signed, and when I answered, my mind was a million miles away from personal problems. But I was abruptly snapped back into them, when Donna said, "Deb? Is that you?"

"Yes, what's wrong? Is Lori worse?"

"No, she seems to be a little better. At least she's been really restless. Deb, the doctor told me something the other day and I've been thinking about it and I wanted to ask you. They've found out that if a comatose person has a dog or cat they're really crazy about, that sometimes the pet can wake them up when a person can't. The doctor asked me if Lori had a pet, and said if she did we'd move her temporarily to a private room and bring the pet in. I told him she didn't have a pet, but I got to thinking today, that dog of yours—"

"Pat, yes. I don't know how much Lori cares about him, but he certainly misses her."

"Then can you bring him to the hospital? The doctor said I need to tell him several hours in advance, so he can arrange to move her to that private room. Of course, they don't want everybody in intensive care to have to cope with somebody's dog."

"I don't think I can get there before you have to leave," I said, "because I'm still on duty and I have a house to search, but—"

"I'm off tonight," Donna said, "so anytime you can get here..."

"I won't promise when," I said, "but I'll be there."

Dutch came back in, the stack of warrants and petitions for warrants in his hand. "You'll be there where?"

"At the hospital. I'm going to take my dog up there."

"Right," Dutch said. "You're going to take your dog to the hospital, and they're going to open the door and let him right in."

"Well, they are. I'll explain in the car."

And explain I did, as Dutch drove to the Huffman house. Then we both put family matters out of our minds.

Perhaps I should have called before coming, to make sure they were back from the funeral. But I have a pretty fair idea how long funerals take, and I certainly didn't want to warn them I was coming.

Perhaps showing up at Clara Huffman's door with a search warrant the same day as her husband's funeral was hitting a little below the belt, but if there was any evidence remaining, how long would it continue to remain?

Mardee Hamilton was standing at the big front window behind open draperies, facing outside, smoking. That wasn't too much of a surprise; and of course she saw us and went to the door to let us in. The big surprise was Clara Huffman, who looked up, in apparent astonishment, at our entrance.

She was not sitting and doing nothing, as she had been doing last time I came to ask questions. She was reading, which wasn't an enormous surprise, as I had already deduced from the number of books that either she or Eric, most likely both, liked to read. What did surprise me was what she was reading—a Xanth novel. If I had been asked to make a list of things I did not expect her to read, I would have probably put a fantasy novel replete with monstrous puns on the bottom of the list.

A fantasy novel that could very well have been the inspiration for the virus that had attacked an entire computer network.

I went and sat down beside her, without saying anything. She looked at me and at the novel and at me and at the novel.

"Yeah, I figured it out," I said. "You have the right to remain silent . . ." After I finished the usual spiel, I asked, "Was it hard to write the virus program?"

"Oh, no," she said, "it was easy. I know a lot about computers. When Eric first got the computer it was going to be for both of us, but then he took it over and spent all his time with it, and there never was time for him to spend with me or time for me to spend working on the computer. So I did a lot more reading about computers, and I studied programming, and then I wrote the virus." She laughed. "I didn't really know it was going to get in a lot of other computers, though. I just meant it to get in Eric's computer. That was kind of funny, though."

"A lot of people didn't think it was a bit funny."

She shrugged. "They were probably neglecting their families, just as Eric was. But the problem, you see, was that the virus didn't stop it. He went right on neglecting me while he tried to cure the virus. I could have told him how to cure the virus, but of course he didn't ask me."

"If he had asked you, would you have told him?"

"I don't know. Maybe I would. I would have pretended to have to figure it out, though. I certainly couldn't have told him I already knew."

I glanced at Mardee. There was no surprise at all on her face. She already knew this; either she had figured it out herself or Clara had at some point confessed it to her.

"What are you going to charge me with?" Clara asked.

"I don't know yet." I really didn't. I hadn't come out here suspecting her of writing a computer virus; I would have thought that was completely beyond her capabilities. But on the other hand, this was the first time I had seen her when she was neither in shock nor under the influence of a tranquilizer; I had no idea when she had stopped taking the Xanax, but I was certain she had stopped. "When Eric went on spending his time with the computer—"

"I broke the computer, of course." Her voice was quite calm. "He was always having things that took time away from me, but most of them he got tired of after a while. The motor home . . . the electric trains . . . the ham radios . . . but every one of them, he'd get tired of in a few months and then he'd come back to me. But the computer . . . he'd had the computer nearly two years and he still wasn't tired of it. It was supposed to be *our* computer and instead it became *his* computer. Obviously the only thing to do about it was break the computer. Break it to where he couldn't fix it." She looked at me. "I'm sure *you* don't understand things like that. Your husband pays attention to you instead of to his hobbies."

"My husband," I said, surprised by the tone of icy anger in my voice, "was one of the other people whose computer you zapped. Right now he's spending about twenty hours a day on the computer. Before that it was ham radios, and he's also had fishing, hunting, camping, electric trains, an airplane we could no more afford than the man in the moon...you name it, he's had it as a hobby, and sometimes I get pretty tired of it. But it certainly has never crossed my mind to kill his computer—or him."

Clara stared at me, totally astonished. "You think I killed *Eric?*"

"Didn't you?"

"Don't you think she ought to have an attorney present before answering that sort of question?" Mardee interrupted.

"*Really,* Mardee!" Clara protested. "Anybody would think you think I *did* murder Eric! No, of course I didn't. I broke the computer and then I went to get my hair done. I did break the computer. But that was all. And I really don't think you're going to be able to charge me with anything, because I do know a *little* about the law, and all I did was put a virus in my husband's computer and that's a domestic matter. If he hadn't gotten onto that network then of course the virus wouldn't have gotten out to the other computers, so that's not my fault at all. And I did break his computer, but that was a domestic matter also."

"Not if he called the police," I said.

"But he didn't," Clara said.

"If you broke the computer and then went to get your hair done, and he was dead when you got back, how do you know he didn't call the police?" I asked.

"He wouldn't," Clara said. "I left the ax in his study so he'd be sure to know it was me. And he wouldn't call the police about me."

"She's right," Mardee said. There was some scorn in her voice. "Eric wouldn't call the police no matter what Clara did."

"Why not?" Dutch asked, from where he was standing not too far from Mardee.

Clara tossed her head in a gesture that was probably quite effective when her hair was much longer. "Because," she said, "Texas is a community property state, and Eric was greedy."

"IT WOULDN'T HAVE done any good," Dutch said, in the car.

"That still didn't give you the right to unilaterally decide we weren't going to search the house."

"You unilaterally decided we were going to search it. Use your head, Deb, okay? What were we going to find? She *gave* us the work sheets with the virus program on them. The ax is in property. We've already got her clothes with blood on them and perfectly good explanations for the blood on the clothes. Let's face it, if she killed her husband, she's gotten away with it, because we're never going to be able to prove it."

"So you're just going to sit there and let somebody get away with murder."

"I don't know that she did it. Neither do you. I do know if she did we can't prove it."

"You've said that about four times."

"You haven't listened to me say it one time. We can't win 'em all. You know that as well as I do."

I was silent for a long time, as Dutch went on driving. Finally I said, "Maybe we can't prove this one, but maybe we can prove the other."

"Which other?"

"Helen."

"What are you talking about? You told me yourself, not two hours ago, that you're sure that one was a copycat crime."

"I know I did. But who did the copycat and why? There has to be a connection between the two, because of Eric's hatchet winding up in the alley behind Helen's Club. And I'm still thinking about what Mardee said."

"What she said about what?"

"About Eric. She said, 'Texas is a community property state, and Eric was greedy.' Okay, what she was saying was that Clara has—or had—grounds for divorce, and Eric didn't want her to use them."

"You don't need grounds for a divorce, or haven't you ever heard of no-fault divorce?"

"You can get a no-fault divorce if both parties agree. But she as much as said Eric wouldn't agree. Which means she would need grounds, if she wanted one."

"Anyway, maybe she was the one that was greedy. What was greedy about Eric wanting to keep the money he earned?"

"I just keep having the feeling there's something I'm missing," I said miserably. "I thought of that once and then we found the ax...the hatchet, I mean. Then I still kept feeling that way and then spotted the computer."

"What?" Dutch said.

"The computer. You know. I told you. One was broken before the killing and one was broken after."

"You're reaching if you think that means a copy-cat killer," Dutch commented, stopping for a red light.

"How so?"

"Simple. If you want to kill somebody and destroy his computer, if he's there to start with you get him first; if he's not there to start with you get the computer first."

That made sense, but I was so tired I didn't want to admit it. There was no real reason for me to be so tired; it wasn't much past noon, but all the same I was.

By golly, I was going to *take* some of that comp time this afternoon. If I was right about who did these two killings—and why—there wasn't any danger to anybody else anyway, and I had to take a dog to a hospital.

Surprise, surprise. A real surprise this time. Captain Millner agreed that I could have some comp time, provided I did a few things first. Just a few things. Minor ones.

So I finished the chart, which only took about half an hour and told me nothing I didn't already know. I collected the decent pictures we had of the two victims—we'd collected them from various times, various places—so that I'd have them ready to work with tomorrow, because I was sure that if I asked the right people the right questions I was going to find the connections I was looking for.

And then I went home, fed Cameron, and put him down for his nap (Harry should have already done that, but he was busy playing catch-up with his homework), fed Harry and me, and put myself down for my nap.

Which, in my opinion, I richly deserved.

I woke up when Hal came banging in from school. Unless he rides home with one of his friends, in which case he's home earlier, or is detained for any reason, in which case he gets home later, the school bus delivers him to the front door at approximately three-forty-five. He comes in and eats a snack—two or three peanut butter sandwiches and a quart or two of milk—before taking off to wherever he's going, which for the last two weeks had of course been the hospital.

"Hal," I said, "they're going to move Lori to a private room today so we can take Pat to visit her, so why don't you wait and go with me when I go?"

"You're going to take the dog to the hospital?" Hal repeated. "How come?"

"The doctor thinks the dog might wake her up."

"Oh, come on," Hal said.

Frankly, I agreed. But if there was even a chance it might work— "Are you going with me?" I repeated.

"No, I'll go on now," he said, "and maybe they'll let me help move her."

Even he knew better than that, but I didn't say so. "Well, get your dirty clothes out of your room and I'll get a load or two of wash done before I go up there."

"Okay," he said. As he tossed his jacket down on the coffee table, a color Polaroid picture fell out.

I picked it up. It was of Lori and Donna and it looked quite recent. "Where'd you get this?" I asked.

"An Armadillo gave it to me." He dashed off in the direction of his room.

I hope I may be pardoned if I looked at my son at that moment as if he had taken total, final, leave of his senses. "An armadillo gave it to you?"

"Ah, Mom," he said disgustedly, pausing at the entrance to the hall. "Not an armadillo. An Armadillo."

The difference between common noun and proper noun was now fairly obvious in his intonation, but I still hadn't the slightest idea what—or who—he was talking about.

"One of those guys," he said. "You know. An Armadillo."

"Hal, will you please explain to me what you mean by an Armadillo?"

He took a deep breath, obviously exasperated at the total obtuseness of adults. "Okay, you remember that Red Beret organization, those urban guerillas, whatever their names were? That Lisa Sliwa or Silwa or whatever her name was came to town about?"

"Yes, I remember them," I said cautiously, "but what does that have to do with Armadillos?"

"Okay, well, teenagers like to go to malls."

"I've noticed that, but what does that have to do with—"

"Okay, and some teenagers go to malls and act like jerks and then the malls don't want any teenagers there because of the jerks."

"Okay, but—"

"Mom, will you let me finish?" he demanded, sounding uncommonly like me when either Harry or Captain Millner keeps interrupting my explanation to demand an explanation.

"Okay," I said. "Sorry. Excuse me. Continue."

"So some teenagers got together and it was kind of a joke in a way, Teenage Mutant Ninja Turtles, so they called themselves Ninja Armadillos—because of armadillos..."

He didn't have to explain that. Texas, last I heard, was still the only state in the United States to have armadillos. At one point the creatures had extended their range north, up into Oklahoma, but then they moved back south again. Personally I do not consider armadillos anything to brag about—they're stupid, they stink, and they carry leprosy—but some people seem quite fond of them.

"...okay, and the Armadillos, when they find kids in the malls acting like jerks, they take pictures of them. And then they find out who they are and send the pictures to them. And tell them if they keep on acting like jerks in the mall then they'll send the pictures to their parents or even to the police, if they're acting like real jerks, you know, shoplifting and stuff like that."

"In other words they indulge in mild blackmail," I said.

"Well, yeah, but what do you want them to do?"

"Hal, I don't especially want them to do anything," I said. "Anyway, what does all that have to do with the Guardian Angels?"

"Well, nothing, really, except that they both want people to behave."

I picked up the picture again. "But surely Lori and Donna weren't acting like jerks."

"No, of course not. This was..." He swallowed. "This was the very day Lori got hit. They, Lori and her mom, went to Tandy Center and to the library both. They'd been doing some, you know, like, shopping, and they'd stopped to get something to eat, and an Armadillo saw them and took their picture just for fun. And he heard a couple of days ago that Lori was still in the hospital and he thought I would want the picture so he went and found it and gave it to me today. At school. And asked me how Lori is doing. I told him I didn't know. That was all I could tell him.''

I picked up the picture again and looked at it. I could recognize the location now—Tandy Center is a downtown mall, which includes a tunnel under one street to the library, a longer tunnel with a trolley shuttle service to a distant parking lot, and a skywalk over another street to a fancy, and expensive, hotel. This picture had been taken at a snack bar on an upper level, not far from the skywalk.

And then I froze, the picture in my hand. Behind Donna and Lori there were several people who apparently had just stepped off the skywalk. Two of them, holding cocktail glasses, their arms wrapped around each other, looked very familiar.

Helen Thorne and Eric Huffman.

I had my connection.

"Hal, I need this picture," I said.

He grabbed at it. "Mom, you can't—"

"Hal, I promise, I will take it straight to Kinko's and have a color copy made and give the original right back to you and I will take good care of it. But

I need this picture. And I need the name and address of the Armadillo who took it and I need to talk to that Armadillo. It is extremely important.''

"You promise I'll get it back?"

"I already promised. What's the name of—?"

"The Armadillo? Oh, I don't remember, but I'll find him at school."

"Please do. And tell him to call me at home or at work, whichever, as soon as possible.'' I put the picture into my billfold. Now if I could just find the police officer who'd gone to the house that day, so that officer could testify that Eric was alive at the time he left . . .

I called dispatch.

They still hadn't found any record of a call.

I telephoned Methodist Hospital.

"They'll have her in the private room by five,'' Donna said. "And they've made the arrangements for bringing the dog in. You just have to stop at the front desk so they can send a security guard in with you, so everybody'll know it's okay."

"I'll be there at five, dog and all,'' I promised, the laundry I was going to do totally forgotten. I looked at my watch. If I left now I might have time to prowl around the Huffman neighborhood a little, to ask questions Dutch wouldn't have known to ask when he was prowling around the day of the killing.

I probably should have taken the time to wash Pat instead, but bathing him never does any good because he instantly rolls in the dirt again. So he might as well go as his own doggy self—and anyway, as many times as Lori had grabbed him by the collar to dog-march him where he did not want to go, that doggy odor was quite familiar to her, and who knows, maybe the smell of the pet was part of what would help to wake her up.

According to Dutch's report, the neighbor who'd reported seeing the police car was one Sharon McCandless, who lived diagonally across the street. I didn't call first. I just went there, leaving Pat whining unhappily in the car with the windows rolled up too far for him to get out but not far enough that he would run any risk of suffocation, though in this weather I didn't think he was in any great danger.

The McCandless house was comfortably elegant, with the look that Clara Huffman probably was striving for and just missing. The look was yuppie, but not aggressively yuppie; the house was well designed, for utility as well as looks, and the furniture was well planned for attractive comfort. My guess was Sharon McCandless, who was probably ten years younger than me, had the money to hire a cook and a maid if she wanted to, but like Becky and Olead, she didn't want to. I pulled up a stool at the breakfast bar and asked questions as she diced onions and bell peppers for the spaghetti she was making. "I wouldn't normally have noticed," she said, "because normally that time of day I'm busy in the house, but I'd been shopping, and I was getting groceries out of the car."

"And the police car parked in front of the Huffman house?"

"That's right." She wiped a stray lock of hair back from her forehead with the back of her hand.

"About what time was this?"

"Oh, call it three, three-fifteen. It was just before the rain started. Why don't you ask the officer? Surely there'd be a report or something."

"I'm sure there is," I said, "but unfortunately it seems to be misplaced, and nobody can figure out what officer it was who came out here that time. And I need to talk to him."

"Her," Mrs. McCandless said.

"Sorry, her. Did you by any chance happen to notice a number on the car?"

"Oh, it wasn't that kind of a police car," Mrs. McCandless said. "Just a car. Kind of small and not real new."

I stared at her in some dismay. This changed the picture completely. Because if it had been an unmarked police car it should have been an ununiformed police officer. A uniformed police officer, in an unmarked car—especially one that was small and not very new—and especially at three or three-fifteen—was a police officer on her way to work, stopping to visit or to carry out some private investigation of her own. That meant there wouldn't be a report. And that meant if the officer didn't re-

alize on her own that I needed to talk with her—
which if she was going to do she would probably already have done—I might need to check with every
uniformed policewoman in Fort Worth and, for that
matter, in many of the other jurisdictions in the
area.

Unless Clara or Mardee could tell me what policewoman might have dropped in to visit with Eric
for about half an hour on the day of his death. As I
had never produced the search warrant and they
didn't know I had it, they might not yet be mad
enough at me to refuse to talk with me.

ELEVEN

MARDEE'S CAR WAS GONE; apparently Clara was now presumed to be fit to drive. I certainly hoped that estimation was correct, because as I walked across the street Clara got out of one gray Lincoln town car she had parked in front of the house, marched back into the garage, and backed a second gray Lincoln town car out, to park it directly behind the first one as I stepped onto the sidewalk.

She got out of the second car and looked at me. "One is mine and one is Eric's," she said. "I'm trying to decide which one I should get rid of. What do you think?"

The two looked virtually identical to me, except that one had a dented fender. "I'd get rid of that one, I guess, if I were you," I said.

"That's what I thought, too. It's Eric's. So I'm keeping mine. Only I don't like it very much either. I think a car should be a pretty color. What do you think?"

"By all means get rid of both of them and get a pretty car, if that's what you want."

"I'm thinking about taking a cruise to the Bahamas. What do you think?"

"I think you'd better learn to decide what you think, instead of asking somebody else. Anyway, you can't leave Fort Worth quite yet."

She looked at me quizzically. "Because you still think I killed Eric?"

"*Somebody* killed Eric," I pointed out.

"I keep telling you it was that awful boy."

"I don't think it was," I said.

"Well, nobody else would have any reason. Now would they?"

I crossed my arms over my breast. "Maybe you had a reason. You were tired of Eric ignoring you, and you wanted an Easter egg car instead of a gray car, and you wanted a cruise to the Bahamas instead of a trip in a motor home to a hamfest."

"I did," Clara said. "But I didn't kill Eric to get them. That would be silly. He's—he was much older than I am, and he had a bad heart. All I had to do was wait."

"That sounds a little cold-blooded."

"Oh, it was," Clara said. "But it was the truth all the same. What are you here about this time? Still trying to find out if I killed Eric? Because if you are, I still didn't."

"Actually, there's something else I'm trying to find out this time," I said.

"Well, what is it? I don't have all day. I have to call the car dealer to come get this dented car."

"What happened to it, by the way?" I asked.

"Is that what you came to ask?"

"No, I just wondered."

Clara looked at the fender. "I don't know. He didn't tell me. If *I* had dented a fender he would have yelled at me about it for a week. 'Women drivers!' But if *he* dented a fender of course he wouldn't tell me about it. I didn't know until I went to get the car out this morning."

"Then maybe he did it when he went to play golf that morning," I suggested.

"He didn't drive to the golf course," Clara said.

"How do you know, if you weren't here?" I asked.

"Because I heard him call Will Eubanks and ask Will to pick him up," Clara said. "That was before I left. Anyway, I was still here when he left. I left about an hour or so later. I don't know when he did it. He hadn't been driving much the last couple of weeks, and when he did he took my car. I thought it was pretty selfish of him. What do you think?"

"Undoubtedly," I said. "Now, what I wanted to ask—"

"Get on to it," Clara said.

I took a deep breath. Oddly enough, I was now finding Clara more likeable than I had earlier; apparently Clara around Mardee and Clara not around Mardee were two somewhat different women. That did not, however, mean that I no longer suspected Clara of murdering her husband; some murderers are perfectly likeable.

"Around three or so," I said, "before you got home, a policewoman in uniform came here and stayed for about half an hour. We need to talk to her but we don't know who it was. We thought at first it was somebody Eric had called, and we were puzzled because we couldn't find any record of a call, but now we've found out it was somebody in her own car, probably on her way to work. So what policewoman did Eric know who might have dropped by to visit on her way to work?"

"Eric didn't know any police," Clara said promptly. "Male or female. All his work was civil and we've just never had any occasion to meet any police. Who told you that anyway? That McCandless woman? I saw you on your way from her house."

"She was one of—"

"Because she's so wrapped up in those children of hers she's liable to see anything whether it's there or not, or *not* see anything whether it's there or not. There wasn't a policewoman here. There was no *reason* for one to be. We don't know any, and Eric wouldn't have called about the computer. He'd have just yelled at me for a few weeks. That's all. That's all he did when—"

She stopped abruptly.

"When what?" I asked.

"When I broke his train set," she disclosed. "He spent too much time with it, too."

"Clara Huffman, you are a very jealous woman," I said.

"He never would let me have children," Clara said. "If he wouldn't let me have children then he owed me some time."

"Did you want children?"

"Well, no," Clara said, "but if he'd wanted me to have them I would have. Now, I've got to go."

"Fine," I said, "and I'll go too." I was back to disliking this highly inconsistent woman.

I'd written down Mardee's address, which wasn't too far away. If anybody knew of Eric's friendship with a policewoman, I thought, it would probably be Mardee anyway, not Clara.

But Mardee Hamilton wasn't home. I'd have to catch her to talk with her tomorrow. Oh, well, it was time for me to get on to the hospital anyway.

I didn't have any trouble taking Pat up to the intensive care floor, once I had, as Donna had instructed, stopped at the front desk to get a security guard escort. Pat trotted fairly docilely beside me, occasionally shying toward my legs and not offering to eat anybody, even the uniformed security guard, and I'll admit I had felt a little nervous about that. He didn't like this place; it smelled too much like the vet's office for him. But as we entered Lori's room Pat suddenly whined and pulled me forward. Even with the smells of the medicines and all the unfamiliar people he'd recognized Lori, and he wanted to get in bed with her. He totally ignored Donna, Hal, and me.

Lori had been detached from most of the wires and tubes for the moment; apparently the hospital had already determined that pets and wires and tubes don't mix too well. Pat put his forepaws on the bed, but he wasn't quite a tall enough dog to get his head up on a high hospital bed. "Can we lower the bed?" I asked Donna.

Before she had time to answer, Hal was lowering the bed. Pat looked extremely startled at the movement and dropped back to the floor until the bed was low enough; then he put his front paws back on the bed along with his head, whined at Lori, and began to lick her face. She turned her head sharply. That was very encouraging.

"I don't want to look," Donna said. "I don't like dogs. I know she does, but I don't." Very determinedly, she said, "I want to talk about something else. How's Harry's school going?"

"Just fine. I don't know much about it."

"How's...uh...how's your case going?"

I shrugged. "Confusing. I thought I knew who did it but now I'm not sure. There was a policewoman who went to the house about three o'clock, and I need to locate her and talk with her. Apparently she wasn't on duty, because she was in her own car, but my witness can't describe it very well. But she was in uniform. Once I talk with her..."

I stopped. Donna was looking at me. Looking at me steadily, with an expression on her face that was absolutely unreadable. And then, suddenly, it all clicked together. Pat at the murder scene, following bloody footprints and trying to get into a police car. A piece of gray paint from the car that had struck Lori. A dented fender on a gray Lincoln in front of the house of a murdered man. A photograph that placed the two victims, drinking, perhaps unfit to drive, within half an hour of the time and place Lori had been struck.

I didn't want to know. I didn't want to be sure. But I did know and I was sure. The car didn't tell me, nor did the paint fragment, or even the photograph, though perhaps it should have.

No, it was Donna herself who told me, with the look on her face, with her sudden unreachable stillness.

"Hal," I said, surprised my voice was holding so steady, "go down to the gift shop and get me a Coke."

"Aw, Mom! Right now? Lori's about to wake up—"

"Right now," I said, and something in my voice must have warned him not to argue further, because he went. As soon as he was out of earshot, I said, "Donna, what have you done?"

"You know what I did," Donna said, turning away from me, looking at the bed where Pat was still licking Lori's face. "I got the license number. And

I started to give it to the investigating officers, but then I thought, No, I won't. The driver'll get off with a slap on the wrist. So then I thought, If Lori wakes up then I'll give the license number to the investigators. But she didn't wake up. She didn't wake up. So finally I ran the license plate number to find out who it belonged to. And then I went over there. I wasn't going to do anything. I was just going to talk to him. That was all, just talk to him. I asked him why he kept going. He said it wouldn't have done any good to stop, and his girlfriend was in the car. I made him tell me who his girlfriend was. He told me...Deb, he told me he was sorry. Sorry for me, sorry for my daughter. Be he said surely I could understand why he didn't stop. He said, 'I want to show you something.' Then he took me in there where his computer was all torn up. He said, 'This is the kind of woman I live with. Look what she did to my computer. If I'd stopped...if she'd known I was with Helen...she'd have more ammunition to use against me. And I saw the way the girl flew when the car hit her. It wouldn't have done any good for me to stop. Surely you can understand that.' He was drinking. He was drinking a lot. Deb, I didn't mean to do anything. I wasn't going to do anything. The hatchet...the hatchet was already in there. I didn't take it in there. I picked it up because he had the most...the most I-don't-care expression on his face I ever saw. And I was so angry...so angry...my husband was dead because of a hit-and-run driver and my daughter was dying and he expected *me* to understand why he didn't stop...and I just started hitting...and it was like I couldn't stop. I didn't mean to kill him. But then after...I got to thinking...if he didn't care any more than that, if he could knock Lori forty feet and not even stop...then he deserved to die...like that...and the woman in the car, his girlfriend, she could have made him stop. It wasn't because they hit Lori. He was DWI and he should have been punished for that, but that wasn't why. It was because they didn't *stop.*"

"So you killed her too."

Donna nodded. "I took the hatchet with me when I left his house, wrapped in a paper bag. I knew when I could catch her at the club alone because I've seen her there lots of times. That's my beat. My beat, while I'm on this shift. Andy Ryan has it after me."

"Yes, I know. That night, he got the same car you'd had."

She smiled sadly. "Leave it to you to notice that."

"I know because I had Pat try to follow the blood trail. He tried to get in the police car. Twice."

Donna looked at Pat, still licking Lori's face. "I never did like dogs. I was sorry Andy had to find it, though. It was a real mess. I figured that boy would report it, but I guess he didn't."

"That boy. Shane. You chased him down the alley that night, and then telephoned him later."

She nodded again. "Hal brought him up here to see Lori. I recognized him then. He didn't recognize me. But he might have, later. I didn't want to hurt him. I wasn't chasing him to hurt him. I just wanted him to go away. That night, and later. That was all." She turned again, to glance at Lori. "They were laughing, in the car."

"Eric and Helen?"

"Yes. Them. I saw them laughing. Just before they hit Lori—they were laughing. So I killed him. And then I killed her and then broke up her computer, the way the other one was. I had a reason to be mad at them but not to be mad at the computers. So I figured that would throw the police off the track. And it would have, if it had been anybody but you."

"That's right. It would have. It threw me off the track. I wouldn't have guessed ... Donna, how did you manage to get to work on time? You must have been covered with blood—"

"I took a shower in my clothes," she said. "Before I left the house, his house. Nobody noticed. It was raining that day, I got to muster soaking wet and fifteen minutes late, and I said I had to walk four blocks from where I left my car. Nobody noticed. It was raining. It rained till four-thirty."

"Donna, what am I going to do now?" I asked painfully. "What am I going to do with you...about you?"

"You don't have to do anything," she said. "I'll do it. I can't go to jail, Deb, you know that. You know what happens to cops in jail."

I did know. But I didn't want to know. "Donna, you could claim justifiable homicide—"

"You know better than that."

She was right. I did know better than that.

But she was still talking. "The first one—maybe. I don't know. Temporary insanity? Maybe it really was. I didn't go there to kill him. I really didn't. I just wanted him to confess. Only—he was being so, he thought, reasonable. I don't even remember...doing it. Just standing there, after, out of breath, still holding the hatchet."

"So you can—"

"No. That one—if it had just been that one— maybe. Only then I wouldn't have a job or any way to get one ever again and what would happen to Lori then? Anyhow—it's the second one. Deb, that was premeditated. Even I know that. You don't have to do anything. Just...take care of Lori. If she wakes up. If she ever wakes up. Don't ever let her know why."

"I'll try," I said. "But Donna—she won't have anybody—"

"She'll have my sister. And Hal. And you. I was a crummy mother anyway."

"Donna—"

"And an even crummier cop." She glanced once more at the bed, where Pat was still trying to wake up Lori, and then, quickly, she walked through the door. I didn't try to stop her. She knew I wouldn't. I wasn't going to fight her in Lori's room, I wasn't going to fight her in the hospital, and I couldn't leave Lori alone, and in the time it would take me to yell for a nurse and get one in here Donna would be gone anyway, so all I could do was watch her go.

Then, from the bed, a soft frail voice said, "Pat? You've got my face all wet... Deb? Is that you? Where am I? What happened?"

So I told her what happened. But not everything, not yet.

When Hal came back with the Coke, I left the Coke on the dresser, left Hal with Lori, and took Pat with me to find Donna.

She was in her car, in the parking terrace. The .38 service revolver had dropped from her pale hand.

HAL WANTED LORI to come and live with us, but he was unexpectedly—and unusually—acquiescent, when her aunt and I agreed that Lori would live with her aunt. After all, the aunt was only three blocks away from us.

Dutch and I went out together to search Donna's house; Irene went with us to look for physical evidence, and Captain Millner went too, to make sure everything was done properly. The uniform, still wet, now moldy and stained, was lying in a heap in the garage, and despite the shower, despite the rain, despite the days of rot and mildew, the luminol test showed the blood spatters clearly. And her uniform shoes, despite the cleaning and polishing she'd given them since then, still had blood in the seams.

A closer examination of the yellow slicker I'd found behind Helen's showed where the black tape that spelled out POLICE had been peeled off the back and where a name tag had been cut out. We couldn't find Donna's slicker at her house, so that had to be it. And the sneakers were Donna's size.

Of course, it was hard for Lori, when we finally told her. Told her what, and finally, why, because she really did have to know. Hal claimed the task, which was good of him, because it couldn't have been any easier for him than it would have been for anybody else. She cried a lot. But Lori's durable; Lori will make it, and she's got a lot of people to lean on, a lot of people who love her.

Captain Millner let me take every bit of my comp time, right at Christmas time, when nobody was supposed to be allowed to take time off. But I never did finish crocheting the Christmas tree, and I don't suppose I ever will. I put up the real Christmas tree for Hal and for Cameron, because this was the first Christmas Cameron had been old enough to notice.

I called Hal's bishop and asked him if I would feel better if I joined the church. He said about this, probably I wouldn't, but I was welcome to join the church anyway. I told him I'd think about it.

I called Susan and asked if she could prescribe me some sort of antidepressant. "No," she said firmly. "Antidepressants are for depression that comes from inside. When you've been through something traumatic, you have to work through it, not block it out. I've been telling you that for years."

That was true. She had. That didn't mean I had to like hearing it. If I could have laid my hands on some Valium I would have taken a lot of it, which is probably why my doctor refused to prescribe it.

I'd even have taken Xanax, if I could have gotten hold of it. Anything at all, to blot out those memories—

But Lori wasn't taking anything. And she was up walking around now, out of the hospital, officially living with her aunt but over at our house all the time, even if she did spend a lot of the time rocking Cameron as long as he'd sit still and consent to be rocked, a lot of the time sitting outside on the picnic table even though it was December, scratching Pat's ears while he wagged his hind-quarters, licked her face, and whined anxiously because he could tell something was wrong even if he didn't know what.

I guess Susan was right. We all had to work through it.

It helped a little, in an odd way, when Shane took off the day before Christmas Eve, taking with him the four presents for him that were under the tree, to go to Wyoming to see if he could get a driver's license there. I hadn't had the heart to throw him out.

Even in Fort Worth it's cold in December. But this had been a bad time to have outsiders in the house.

The whole family, including Lori, went for Christmas dinner over to Olead and Becky's house, because Becky said with two in diapers it was easier for her to make dinner than it was to haul the babies somewhere else. That's probably true. I cuddled my first granddaughter awhile.

Then Vickie said she'd take Cameron to spend the night with Barry. I guess when he's older Cameron will think it's funny that he has a nephew older than he is, but he's not old enough to think about that sort of thing yet. He just knows he likes to play with Barry.

Harry took me home. I don't know what he did the rest of the evening. Hal and Lori took Pat for a walk. I sat down in my chair in the living room, and Rags crawled into my lap and started purring. I brushed Rags, and I cried a lot.

HARLEQUIN®

INTRIGUE®

Valentine's Day was the best day of the year for
Dee's Candy and Gift Shop. Yet as the day drew closer,
Deanna Donovan became the target of
malicious, anonymous pranks.

A red heart was pinned to her front door with a dagger.

Dead roses adorned her car.

Soon, she was being stalked by her unseen admirer.

Suspicious of everyone, Deanna has nowhere to turn—and no
way to escape when she is kidnapped and held captive by her
Valentine lover....

#262

Cupid's Dagger
by *Leona Karr*
February 1994

You'll never again think of Valentine's Day without feeling a
thrill of delight...and a chill of dread! CUPID

Caught in the Shadows

C. A. Haddad

STRANGER THAN FICTION

Hacking may be borderline legal, but the profit is there, big-time, especially in a high-profile divorce case such as the one Chicago computer "researcher" Becky Belski has just been handed.

Arrest record? Bank statement? Charges? If it's in a computer network, Becky can find it. What she didn't expect to find was a link to her own murky half-forgotten past...and the murder of her stepfather.

An open-and-shut case convicted Becky's mother more than twenty years ago. Now Becky is certain that the wrong person went to jail. Between hacking away at the past and juggling two men, she finally discovers the shocking truth.

"The hallmark of the C. A. Haddad mysteries...is that they're sassy, sexy and very funny."—*Publishers Weekly*

Available in February at your favorite retail stores.

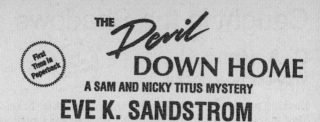

THE *Devil*
DOWN HOME
A SAM AND NICKY TITUS MYSTERY
EVE K. SANDSTROM

First Time in Paperback!

ALL HALLOW'S EVIL

Spotting Dracula hitchhiking at the side of the road, Sheriff Sam Titus and his wife, Nicky, do the neighborly thing—give him a lift. Black cloak and deathly pallor aside, the stranger's name is Damon Revels, and his business in Holton goes back fifteen years.

But trick or treat turns deadly when Damon's body is found in a coffin at the local Haunted House fund-raiser. Surrounding the knife protruding from his chest is a pentagram—the mark of devil worshipers. A human sacrifice?

Then another murder with satanic trimmings occurs, and terror is mounting. Whether it actually is a cult or the work of a clever killer, Sam and Nicky are now hunting the devil down home.

"I'm looking forward to more from Nicky and Sam...a fun, quick read."
—*Mystery News*

Available in March at your favorite retail stores.

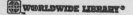

BLOODY TEN

WILLIAM LOVE

First Time In Paperback

PRODIGAL SON

So the unofficial partnership of a cynical New York private eye and a cantankerous Catholic bishop was strange—especially since this nice Jewish gumshoe moonlighted as a clerk for the archdiocese. But it paid the bills. And when one of Davey Goldman's cases got too tough, he pulled in the heavy muscle: the bishop loved putting his brainpower—all 220 IQ points—on the matter.

When Jim Kearney's long-lost brother, Nick, comes looking for trouble, he asks Davey to mediate. But before Davey can earn his money, Nick is dead—and Davey has committed the slightly illegal act of shielding the number-one suspect...his client. He's not above dodging the cops or falling in love with his client's girlfriend, either. Just don't tell the bishop.

"A well-developed cast, tightly structured plot and cleverly placed details end with the bishop's questions in an 11th-hour, nail-biting conclusion."

—*Publishers Weekly*